U0023970

FITTING IN IN CHINESE

遊學華語

文藻外語大學　華語中心

目　錄

序

　　《遊學華語》的教材課本在整體設計上，很有數位教學上的效果，新穎有變化，也給台灣華語文教材增加了新頁。

　　課本內容生活化，達到實際運用的效果。各對話後有「生詞」註解包括：發音、詞類、英譯、例句等。「生詞用法」填空呈現其後，達到了練習的目的。「語法」也配合了句子練習，達成熟練的目的。

　　本書設計之「漢字」古錢方式頗有創意，因「合詞」是華語語言中常用的單位，可養成學習者斷詞的基本習慣。

　　練習中「說說看」，蜜蜂窩的圖形在互動式光碟上的形式十分具有趣味性遊戲的效果。「停看聽」的短文內容，置錄於互動式光碟中讓學生練習聽力，是現代華語教學必備的教學方法。

　　現代第二語言教學重視的是「從做中學」有效率中文的功能，本書編纂方面已儘量達成此一目的。在此世界各地重視華語文教學之際出版一本實用的華語文教材，十分值得慶幸。

國立台灣師範大學
華語文教學研究所
葉德明

內 容 說 明

《遊學華語》一書適用於中級程度的外籍學生。

全冊十二課，每課分為九個部分：對話、生詞、生詞用法、語法、漢字、練習、簡體對照、漢語拼音以及英文翻譯（另有德文翻譯本）。每四課各有一閱讀短文與複習篇。書末附錄有菜單、飲料單、如何查字典等重要資料。全書以幽默生動的插圖貫穿書中的六位中、外籍主角，以答客問的方式增強學習者的理解力。本教材適用於課室內或學生自學，延伸內容製作成光碟，具備聲音與影像功能。可以單獨使用書本或配合多媒體數位學習。

一、【對話】

以角色扮演方式介紹情境，
學生看圖提出問答，
以互動方式進入該課主題。

德美：台灣的交通方便嗎？
老師：大都市都很方便，
　　　　鄉下就不一定了。
歐福：我看每家都有摩托車。

二、【生詞】

重在語用，簡短說明後即做問答練習。

	生詞	簡體字	詞類	拼音	英譯
例	福氣	福气	N.	fúqi	happy and lucky

三、【生詞用法】

緊接在生詞後，現學現用，印象深刻。

例：父母健康，孩子聽話，你真是有＿＿＿！

四、【語法】

四個語法點不多不少，學生練習完課本再視程度做前後的展延，如為什麼？怎麼了？後來忙到幾點？等等。

例：本來…，後來…
問：你本來要去哪裡？
答：我本來要去中國大陸，後來決定來台灣。
　　1.你不是今天沒事嗎？　　沒事/忙死了
　　2.你不是只要一個包子嗎？　要一個/要了兩個
　　3.你不是要去逛街嗎？　　去逛街/去看了電影

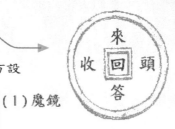

五、【漢字】 ●●

強調華語文的表達多用合詞，透過古錢外圓內方設計，讓學生一窺合詞的妙用。

(1) 魔鏡

六、【練習】 ●●

多種綜合練習，如魔鏡、重組、說說看、連連看、猜猜看、數來寶以及看圖說故事等，激發學生聯想，熟悉中文溝通技巧的同時，擴展對華人社會文化的瞭解。

(2) 重組

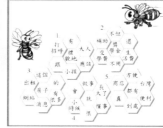

七、【簡體對話】 ●●

八、【拼音對照】 ●●

華語聲調圖

九、【英文翻譯】 ●●

配合各地不同的需求，備有上三項簡體字、漢語拼音、英文翻譯於課末供參酌或延伸教學活動用。

「中文不難，
　　只是不同！」

文藻外語大學　華語中心
　　　　　　　龔三慧

第一課　一二三 到台灣

【一·對話】

（1）介紹台灣

德美：　老師，請問台灣是一個什麼地方？

老師：　台灣是一個人很多，地方不大的海島。

得中：　台灣有多少人口？

老師：　大約有 2300 萬人。

歐福：　台灣人說什麼話？

老師：　多數人說華語和台語，也有不少人會說英文。

（2）為什麼來台灣？

德美： 有人會說德文嗎？

老師： <u>有是有，可是很少</u>，要看他們是做什麼工作。

得中： 台灣有很多外國人嗎？

老師： <u>最近幾年越來越多了</u>。

歐福： 他們來台灣做什麼呢？

老師： <u>有的人來工作，有的人來觀光，也有的人來學中文。</u>

德美： 他們來台灣的目的是什麼？

老師： 有的是因為工作上的需要；有的是因為做生意；有的很單純，他們就是<u>對中國文化、語言有興趣</u>。

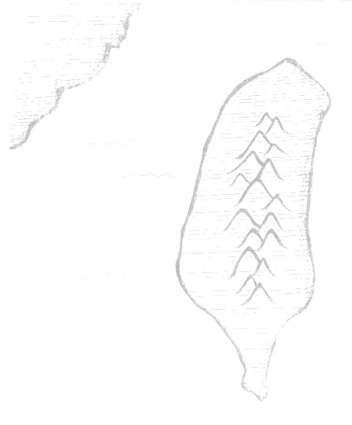

	生詞	簡體字	詞類	拼音	英譯
1.	請問	请问	VP.	qǐngwèn	May I ask…?, Excuse me…
2.	地方	地方	N.	dìfāng	place
3.	海島	海岛	N.	hǎidǎo	island
4.	人口	人口	N.	rénkǒu	population
5.	大約	大约	Adv.	dàyuē	about, approximately
6.	華語	华语	N.	Huáyǔ	Mandarin Chinese
7.	英文	英文	N.	Yīngwén	English
8.	最近	最近	Adv.	zuìjìn	recently
9.	工作	工作	N.	gōngzuò	work, job
10.	觀光	观光	N. V.	guānguāng	tour, tourism
11.	中文	中文	N.	Zhōngwén	Chinese
12.	目的	目的	N.	mùdì	goal, purpose, destination
13.	需要	需要	N. V.	xūyào	need
14.	生意	生意	N.	shēngyì	business, trade
15.	單純	单纯	Adj.	dānchún	pure, simple
16.	文化	文化	N.	wénhuà	culture
17.	興趣	兴趣	N.	xìngqù	interest

【三‧生詞用法】

請填入適當的生詞

1. 問問題以前，一定要先說_____。

2. 這個_____的四周都是海嗎?

3. 這些都是要注意的_____。

4. 這只是一個_____的數字。

5. 這裡有多少_____?

6. 他_____改變了很多。

7. 台灣大多數的人都說_____。

8. 這是一個非常好的_____機會。

9. 我的同事是外國人，我需要跟他說_____。

10. 他們是從香港來台灣_____的觀光客。

11. 學中文是我來台灣的_____。

12. 很多外國人來台灣學_____。

13. 這件事情不太_____。

14. 我_____一份好工作。

15. _____人要和氣生財。

16. 對不起，我沒有_____。

17. 我覺得學語言一定要學_____。

【四‧語法】

（1）…（倒）是…可是…

問：有人會說德文嗎？　答：有倒是有，可是很少數。
　1. 這家店的東西好嗎？　　　好／有點貴
　2. 日本的東西貴嗎？　　　　貴／比較好
　3. 你最近工作忙嗎？　　　　忙／很開心

（2）…越來越…

問：最近怎麼樣？　答：我最近越來越忙。
　1. 你最近工作怎麼樣？　　　工作／多
　2. 你父母最近好嗎？　　　　生活／簡單
　3. 你學中文學得怎麼樣？　　對學中文／有興趣

（3）有的…有的…

問：每個人都會說英文嗎？　答：有的人會，有的人不會。
　1. 留學生畢了業都回國嗎？　回國／留下來工作
　2. 台灣人都說華語嗎？　　　華語／台語
　3. 這裡的人都很和氣嗎？　　和氣／不和氣

（4）對…很有興趣

問：你對什麼有興趣？　答：我對學語言很有興趣。
　1. 做生意
　2. 傳統中國字
　3. 這份工作

【五·漢字】

1. 土地田方圖

2. 國台語言文

3. 外本國際外

字 ➡ 詞 ➡ 句 ➡ 文

1 地	土地	這是我出生、成長的**土地**。
	田地	這塊**田地**以前種米，現在種玉米。
	地圖	看**地圖**就不會迷路了。
	地方	你要去什麼**地方**？ 你知道地址嗎？

　　這一大片**土地**從前都是**田地**，有種菜的、種米的、種玉米的，現在都蓋了大樓，你爺爺小時候住過的**地方**，在**地圖**上都換新名字了。

2 語	國語	**國語**是一個國家的語言。
	台語	用注音符號學**台語**也可以。
	語文	**語文**是語言和文字的合稱。
	語言	**語言**是人說出來的話。

　　來台灣學**國語**或是**台語**，這兩種**語言**都合適。 如果你對中國**語文**有興趣，也想學寫文字的話，那麼學國語就比較方便了。

3 國	外國	春天**外國**觀光客很多。
	本國	**本國**就是你自己的國家。
	國際	最近來台灣的**國際**學生越來越多了。
	國外	有機會應該到**國外**去看看。

　　到**國外**留學，有很多機會認識其他的**國際**學生，跟當地學生、**外國**學生練習說話，語言可以進步得很快，不要常跟**本國**學生在一起說自己的語言。

【六·練習】

（1）連連看

學

做

找

生意　作文
中文　工作　功課
房子　語文
家事
外語
開車
晚飯　東西
老師
說話　朋友

（2）重組

1.
在台灣　再　出國
學好　留學
先　外文

2.
海島　去
多的　我喜歡　到
旅行　國家

3.
工作　我的
是　做生意
我的　也是
興趣　也是

4.
到國外　也是
學習　觀光　目的
是　遊學　的

5.
很少　天氣好
不多　地方　人口
下雨　這個

(3) 看圖說故事

蔡光輝 攝

1. 烏龜跑得越來越快。
2. 澎湖是在台灣西方的小島。
3. 漂亮的海邊,國內外都有。
4. 我對孔子的學說和孔廟都很有興趣。
5. 有的人想學寫毛筆字,有的人想學西方水彩畫。

（1）介绍台湾
德美：老师，请问台湾是一个什么地方？
老师：台湾是一个人很多，地方不大的海岛。
得中：台湾有多少人口？
老师：大约有 2300 万人。
欧福：台湾人说什么话？
老师：多数人说华语和台语，也有不少人会说英文。

（2）为什么来台湾？
德美：有人会说德文吗？
老师：有是有，可是很少，要看他们是做什么工作。
得中：台湾有很多外国人吗？
老师：最近几年越来越多了。
欧福：他们来台湾做什么呢？
老师：有的人来工作，有的人来观光，也有的人来学中文。
德美：他们来台湾的目的是什么？
老师：有的是因为工作上的需要；有的是因为做生意；有的
　　　很单纯，他们就是对中国文化、语言有兴趣。

【八 · 拼音對照】

DÌ YĪ KÈ　　YĪÈRSĀN DÀO TÁIWĀN

（1）Jièshào Táiwān
　Déměi:　　Lǎoshī, qǐngwèn Táiwān shì yíge shéme dìfāng?
　Lǎoshī:　　Táiwān shì yíge rén hěnduō, dìfāng búdà de hǎidǎo.
　Dézhōng:　Táiwān yǒu duōshǎo rénkǒu?
　Lǎoshī:　　Dàyuē yǒu 2,300 wàn rén.
　Ōufú:　　　Táiwān rén shuō shénme huà?
　Lǎoshī:　　Duōshù rén shuō Huáyǔ hàn Táiyǔ, yěyǒu bùshǎo
　　　　　　　rén huì shuō Yīngwén.

(2) Wèishéme Lái Táiwān?

Déměi:　　　Yǒurén huì shuō Déwén ma?

Lǎoshī:　　　Yǒushìyǒu, kěshì hěn shǎo, yàokàn tāmen shì zuò shéme gōngzuò.

Dézhōng:　　Táiwān yǒu hěnduō wàiguó rén ma?

Lǎoshī:　　　Zuìjìn jǐnián yuèlái yuèduō le.

Ōufú:　　　　Tāmen lái Táiwān zuò shéme ne?

Lǎoshī:　　　Yǒude rén lái gōngzuò, yǒude rén lái guānguāng, yě yǒude rén lái xué Zhōngwén.

Déměi:　　　Tāmen lái Táiwān de mùdì shì shéme?

Lǎoshī:　　　Yǒude shì yīnwèi gōngzuò shàng de xūyào, yǒude shì yīnwèi zuò shēngyì, yǒude hěn dānchún, tāmen jiùshì duì Zhōngguó wénhuà, yǔyán yǒu xìngqù.

【九 · 英文翻譯】

◆ **Dialogue** – p. 1~2

(1) International Students' First Visit to Taiwan

Demei:　　　Excuse me, Teacher. What kind of place is Taiwan?

Teacher:　　Taiwan is a small island with a large population.

Dezhong:　　How many people live in Taiwan?

Teacher:　　There are about 23,000,000 people in Taiwan.

Oufu:　　　　What languages do people in Taiwan speak?

Teacher:　　Most people speak Mandarin and Taiwanese, and a lot of people can speak English.

(2) Why Do People Come to Taiwan?

Demei:　　　Can anyone speak German?

Teacher:　　A few people do, but not so many. It depends on their jobs.

Dezhong:　　Are there a lot of people from other countries in Taiwan?

Teacher:　　More and more, recently.

Oufu:　　　　What are they doing in Taiwan?

Teacher:　　Some come to work, some come to travel, and some come to study Chinese.

Demei: Why do they come to Taiwan?

Teacher: They come to study Chinese. Some for their work, some to do business, while others are simply interested in Chinese culture and language.

◆ Vocabulary – p. 3~4

1.	May I ask…? , Excuse me…	Before asking a question, you have to say "Qing wen".
2.	island	This island is surrounded by the sea.
3.	place	These are some of the "little places" you must pay attention to.
4.	about, approximately	This is just an approximate number.
5.	population	What is the population here?
6.	recently	He's changed a lot recently.
7.	Mandarin Chinese	Most of the people in Taiwan speak Mandarin.
8.	work, job	This is a very good job opportunity.
9.	English	My colleagues are foreigners, so I need to speak English with them.
10.	tour, tourism	They are Hong Kong tourists visiting Taiwan.
11.	goal, purpose, destination	My purpose in coming to Taiwan is to study Chinese.
12.	Chinese	Many foreigners come to Taiwan to study Chinese.
13.	pure, simple	This matter is not simple.
14.	need	I need a good job.
15.	business, trade	For a businessman to get rich, he must be friendly.
16.	interest	I'm sorry, I have no interest.
17.	culture	I feel that when learning a language, you must also learn the culture.

◆ Grammar – p. 5

(1) Q: Can anybody speak German? **A:** There are some, but not too many.
1. They are good, but a little too expensive.
2. They are expensive, but they are better.
3. I am busy, but very happy.

(2) Q: How are you lately?　**A:** I'm getting busier, lately.
1. The work load is getting heavier.
2. Senior citizens' lives get more and more simple.
3. I am more and more interested in Chinese.

(3) Q: Does everybody speak English?　**A:** Some do, some don't.
1. As soon as summer arrives, some people go back to their own countries, and some go abroad.
2. Some people speak Mandarin, and some speak Taiwanese.
3. Some people are very friendly, and some aren't.

(4) Q: What are you interested in?
　 A: I'm interested in learning languages.
1. I'm interested in business.
2. I'm interested in traditional Chinese characters.
3. I'm interested in this job.

◆ Word to Sentence – p. 6

1 地	land	This is the land where I was born and grew up.
	field	This field used to be planted with rice, but now it's planted in corn.
	map	Looking at a map, you can't get lost.
	place	Which place do you want to go to?　Do you know the address?

This large piece of land was formerly fields, planted with vegetables, rice and corn.　Now it's covered with buildings.　The places from your grandfather's childhood have all had their names changed on the map.

2 語	Mandarin	Mandarin is a nation's language.
	Taiwanese	It is also possible to use Mandarin Phonetic Symbols to learn Taiwanese.
	language	"Language" includes both written and spoken language.
	spoken language	Spoken language is what we say.

Come to Taiwan to study Mandarin or Taiwanese – both are "OK". But, if you're interested in written Chinese and want to learn to write characters, then Mandarin is more convenient.

3 國	foreign	There are more foreign tourists in the spring.
	one's own country	"Ben guo" just means "your own country".
	international	Recently, more and more international students have been coming to Taiwan.
	overseas	If you have an opportunity, you should go abroad to see the world.

Going abroad to study provides a lot of opportunities to know other international students as well as local students.　This allows you to improve your language skills very quickly, so you shouldn't always stay around students from your own country.

第二課　介紹

(1) 自我介紹

老師：　來來來，我給你們介紹一下，這三位是從德國來的
　　　　同學。

歐福：　你好，<u>我是歐福，歐洲的歐、福氣的福</u>。

德美：　你好，我是德美，德國的德、美國的美。

得中：　你好，我叫得中，得到的得、中文的中。

小文：　你們好，我是王玉文，你們可以叫我小文。

阿山：　大家好，我是金貝山，你們可以叫我阿山。

（2）學中文

小文： 你們的中文都說得很好，學多久了？
德美： 我跟得中一樣，學了一年多。
歐福： 我學了兩年了，可是還是不太好。
阿山： 你太客氣了！
老師： 他們已經認識很多簡體字了，現在來台灣學正體字。
阿山： 哇！小文，你看得中寫的中國字，比我寫得還漂亮。
得中： 謝謝你，阿山，可是不可能吧！
小文： 有可能，得中，你看看阿山的作業，就知道了！

【二·生詞】

	生詞	簡體字	詞類	拼音	英譯
1.	介紹	介绍	V.	jièshào	introduction(s), introduce
2.	同學	同学	N.	tóngxué	school mate(s)
3.	歐洲	欧洲	N.	Ōuzhōu	Europe
4.	福氣	福气	N.	fúqì	happiness and good fortune
5.	得到	得到	N.	dédào	to succeed in attaining
6.	大家	大家	N.	dàjiā	everybody
7.	多久	多久	Adj.	duōjiǔ	how long
8.	一樣	一样	Adj.	yíyàng	the same, alike
9.	還是	还是	Adv.	háishì	still, yet
10.	客氣	客气	Adj.	kèqì	polite
11.	認識	认识	V.	rènshì	to know, recognize
12.	簡體字	简体字	N.	jiǎntǐ zì	simplified characters
13.	正體字	正体字	N.	zhèngtǐ zì	traditional characters
14.	漂亮	漂亮	Adj.	piàoliàng	pretty, beautiful
15.	不可能	不可能	Adj.	bù kěnéng	impossible
16.	作業	作业	N.	zuòyè	homework, schoolwork

【三・生詞用法】

請填入適當的生詞

1. 俗語說：「做好事，可以_____好報。」

2. 他是我的同班_____。

3. 你去過_____哪幾個國家？

4. 你們來台灣_____了？

5. _____ 都有車票了嗎？

6. 請新來的同學自我_____一下。

7. 父母健康，孩子聽話，你真是有_____！

8. 我們是好朋友，可是我們的想法不太_____。

9. 不要_____！你自己點愛吃的，我請客。

10. _____跟簡體字的差別不太大。

11. 用刀子喝湯，那是_____的事情！

12. 我不知道你們已經_____很久了。

13. 他說了很多次，我_____聽不懂。

14. 昨天的_____ 做好了，就給老師。

15. 她不但人客氣，字也寫得很_____。

16. 學了正體字，再學_____，就很容易了。

【四・語法】

(1) …的…，…的…

問：請問「事先」那兩個字怎麼寫？
答：事情的事，先生的先。
   1. 早晚
   2. 得意
   3. 拿手

(2) …得…，是…的？

問：你的中文說得很好，是在哪裡學的？答：是在台灣學的。
   1. 彈吉他／很好　　是跟誰學的？
   2. 寫漢字／很漂亮　是怎麼學的？
   3. 游泳／很快　　　是誰教你的？

(3) …跟…一樣

問：你要吃什麼東西？答：我要吃跟她一樣的東西。
   1. 點／菜
   2. 開／車
   3. 做／練習

(4) …了…了，可是還是不(太)…

問：你學中文多久了？
答：學了一年多了，可是還是不(太)會說。
   1. 住台灣／熟
   2. 用電腦畫畫／會用
   3. 坐公車上學／習慣

【五・漢字】

1.

2.

3.

字⇨　詞⇨　句⇨　文

1 福	口福	我很有**口福**，常吃到好吃的東西。
	幸福	家人都在一起，很**幸福**！
	福星	**福星**是一個能帶來好運的人。
	福氣	我們這一代的人很有**福氣**。

　　朋友都說我是一個很有**福氣**的人，把我當作是他們的**福星**，有好吃的東西一定找我，我真是有**口福**！其實，你只要每天心存感謝，就會覺得自己太**幸福**了！

2 得	心得	你讀了這本書的**心得**是什麼？
	免得	多穿一件衣服**免得**感冒。
	得意	孩子的成就是父母最**得意**的事情。
	得到	這件事讓我**得到**了一個很好的經驗。

　　去旅行的時候，每天把旅遊**心得**寫下來，**免得**忘記那些開心、**得意**的事情，或是**得到**別人幫助的美好記憶。

3 經	已經	我**已經**做完功課了。
	曾經	他**曾經**是一位船長。
	經過	我每天上學都要**經過**這裡。
	經常	你**經常**遲到很不應該。

　　她的工作需要**經常**出國，**曾經**有一個月出國了五次，她說**已經**習慣了。有一次，早上從機場到公司開會，下午開完會又要出差，**經過**家門兩次都沒時間回家看看！

（1）說說看

她最好	把上衣拉上來	一點，不要穿太低。
她最好	多穿	一點，不要穿太少。
她最好	穿 裙子	，不要穿短褲。
她最好	穿 長褲	，不要穿短褲。
他最好	穿 鞋子	，不要穿拖鞋。

 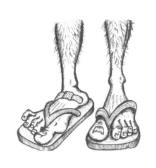 

我不會	穿	拖鞋	去	上課，因為不禮貌。
我不會	穿	牛仔褲	去	參加婚禮，因為不禮貌。
我不會	穿	短褲	去	開會，因為不合適。
我不會	穿	太性感的衣服	去	教堂，因為不合適。
我不會	穿	比基尼泳裝	去	逛街，因為不合適。
我不會	穿	長裙	去	爬山，因為不方便。
我不會	穿	高跟鞋	去	爬山，因為不方便。

（2）看圖說故事

馮超 攝

1. 我就是我。
2. 我跟你的想法不一樣。
3. 我要跟大家介紹一個新商品。
4. 修理了三天了，可是還是不行。
5. 這個小寶寶才剛學游泳，還游得不太好。

（1）自我介绍

老师： 来来来，我给你们介绍一下，这三位是从德国来的
　　　 同学。

欧福： 你好，<u>我是欧福，欧洲的欧、福气的福</u>。

德美： 你好，我是德美，德国的德、美国的美。

得中： 你好，我叫得中，得到的得、中文的中。

小文： 你们好，我是王玉文，你们可以叫我小文。

阿山： 大家好，我是金贝山，你们可以叫我阿山。

（2）学中文

小文： <u>你们的中文都说得很好，学多久了</u>？

德美： <u>我跟得中一样</u>，学了一年多。

欧福： <u>我学了两年了，可是还是不太好</u>。

阿山： 你太客气了！

老师： 他们已经认识很多简体字了，现在来台湾学正体字。

阿山： 哇！小文，你看得中写的中国字，比我写得还漂亮。

得中： 谢谢你，阿山，可是不可能吧！

小文： 有可能，得中，你看看阿山的作业，就知道了！

【八 · 拼音對照】

DÌ ÈR KÈ　　JIÈ SHÀO

（1）Zìwǒ Jièshào

Lǎoshī:　 Lái lái lái, wǒ gěi nǐmen jièshào yí xià, zhè sānwèi
　　　　　 shì cóng Déguó lái de tóngxué.

Ōufú:　　 Nǐhǎo, wǒ shì Ōufú, Ōuzhōu de ōu, fúqì de fú.

Déměi:　　Nǐhǎo, wǒshì Déměi, Déguó de dé, Měiguó de měi.

Dézhōng: Nǐhǎo, wǒ jiào Dézhōng, dédào de dé, Zhōngwén de
　　　　　 zhōng.

Xiǎowén: Nǐmen hǎo, wǒshì Wáng Yùwén, nǐmen kěyǐ jiào wǒ
            Xiǎowén.
Āshān: Dàjiā hǎo, wǒshì Jīn Bèishān, nǐmen kěyǐ jiào wǒ
            Āshān.

(2) Xué Zhōngwén
Xiǎowén: Nǐmen de Zhōngwén dōu shuō de hěn hǎo, xué
            duōjiǔ le?
Déměi: Wǒ gēn Dézhōng yíyàng, xué le yìnián duō.
Ōufú: Wǒ xué le liǎngnián le, kěshì háishì bú tài hǎo.
Āshān: Nǐ tài kèqì le!
Lǎoshī: Tāmen yǐjīng rènshì hěn duō jiǎntǐ zì le, xiànzài lái
            Táiwān xué zhèngtǐ zì.
Āshān: Wa! Xiǎowén, nǐ kàn Dézhōng xiě de Zhōngguó zì,
            bǐ wǒ xiě de hái piàoliàng.
Dézhōng: Xièxie nǐ, Āshān, kěshì bù kěnéng ba!
Xiǎowén: Yǒu kěnéng, Dézhōng, nǐ kànkàn Āshān de zuòyè,
            jiù zhīdào le!

【九・英文翻譯】

◆ **Dialogue** – p. 14~15

(1) Introducing Oneself
Teacher: Come here and let me introduce you. These three students come
            from Germany.
Oufu: Hello, my name is Oufu – the "Ou" in "Europe" (Ou Zhou) and
            the "Fu" in "Happy & Lucky" (fuqi).
Demei: Hello, my name is Demei – the "De" in "Germany" (De Guo)
            and the "Mei" in "America" (Mei Guo).
Dezhong: Hello, my name is Dezhong – the "De" in "Succeed in
            attaining" (dedao) and the "Zhong" in "Chinese" (Zhongwen).
Xiaowen: Hello, my name is Wang Yuwen, but you can call me
            "Xiaowen".

Ashan: Hello everybody, my name is Jin Beishan, and you can call me
            Ashan.

(2) How Long Have You Studied Chinese?

Xiaowen: You all speak Chinese so well, how long have you been
            studying it?

Demei: Like Dezhong, I've been studying for over a year.

Oufu: I've studied Chinese for two years, but I'm still not very good
            at it.

Ashan: You are too modest! (Literally: You are too polite!)

Teacher: They already know many simplified Chinese characters, and
            now that they've come to Taiwan they can learn traditional
            characters.

Ashan: Wow! Look, Xiaowen! Dezhong's written Chinese is more
            beautiful than mine!

Dezhong: Thank you, Ashan, but that's impossible!

Xiaowen: It's possible, Dezhong. Just look at Ashan's homework, and
            you'll know!

◆ Vocabulary – p. 16~17

1.	to achieve	We have a saying, "No good deed shall go unrewarded."
2.	school mate(s)	He's my school mate, in the same class as me.
3.	Europe	How many European countries have you been to?
4.	how long	How long have you been in Taiwan?
5.	everybody	Does everyone have a bus ticket?
6.	introduction(s)	Will the new students please introduce themselves?
7.	happy and lucky	"Parents are healthy and children are well-behaved." You are really fortunate!
8.	the same, alike	We are good friends, but our ways of thinking are not much alike.
9.	polite	Don't be polite! Order whatever you like – it's my treat!

10.	traditional characters	The differences between simplified and traditional Chinese characters are not that great.
11.	impossible	Using a knife to drink soup is just impossible!
12.	to know, recognize	I didn't know you've already known each other for a long time.
13.	still, yet	He has said it many times, but I still don't understand.
14.	homework, schoolwork	As soon as you've finished yesterday's homework, hand it in to the teacher.
15.	pretty, beautiful	She is not only polite, but she also writes Chinese very beautifully, too.
16.	simplified characters	After you learn traditional characters, simplified characters will become easier to learn.

◆ Grammar – p. 18

(1) Q: Excuse me, how do you write the characters for "beforehand"?

　　A: The "shi" of "shiqing" (business), and the "xian" of "xiansheng" (sir, mister).

1. Sooner or later
2. Be satisfied, very successful
3. To be skillful at

(2) Q: You speak Chinese very well, where did you learn it?

　　A: I learned it in Taiwan.

1. Play guitar / well / who did you learn it from?
2. Write Chinese characters / very beautifully / How did you learn that?
3. Swim / very well / who taught you?

(3) Q: What would you like to eat?　　**A:** I'd like to eat what she's having.

1. To order / food
2. To drive / car
3. To do / drill

(4) Q: How long have you studied Chinese?

  A: I've been studying for more than a year, but I still can't speak it very well.

  1. Live in Taiwan /familiar
  2. Using computers to draw /to use very well
  3. Ride the bus to school / used to

◆ Word to Sentence – p. 19

1 福	luck in having good food	I really have luck in getting delicious food, and often have good things to eat.
	happiness, blessing	When the family is all together, that is a blessing!
	lucky star, good luck charm	A "lucky star" is someone who is able to bring good luck.
	good luck	This generation has really been lucky.

My friends all say I'm a lucky person, and think of me as their "lucky star". When they have something good to eat, they always find me to share it with them. I really have good luck with delicious food! Actually, if your heart is thankful every day, you'll find yourself to be blessed by fortune!

2 得	what one gains from an experience, a book, or a movie	What did you gain by reading that book?
	avoid	Wear more to avoid getting a cold.
	proud, satisfied, smug, complacent	Children's successes are parents' greatest satisfaction.
	to obtain	I have gained a lot of experience from this business.

When traveling, one should record one's impressions each day, so as to remember the happy experiences, or the pleasant memories of the kindness of strangers.

3 經	already	I have already finished my homework.
	to have been, formerly	He used to be a ship's captain.
	to pass by	I pass by here daily on my way to school.
	often	You really shouldn't be late so often.

Her work often requires her to travel abroad, and she once had to travel five times in one month.　She says she's already used to it.　One morning she went directly from the airport to a meeting in the office, and after finishing the meeting in the afternoon had to leave again.　On that day, she had passed by her family's house twice, but didn't have time to stop and look in on them!

第三課　飲食文化

【一·對話】

(1) 逛夜市

德美：　好飽喔！我什麼東西也吃不下了！

歐福：　我很想試試所有的小吃，可是真的沒辦法了。

得中：　我們的眼睛比我們的肚子大。

德美：　夜市裡吃的東西真的好多啊！

歐福：　眼睛來不及看，嘴巴也來不及吃。

得中：　老師也來不及說。

老師：　沒關係，改天再請小文帶你們出來，慢慢看、慢慢吃。

（2）請客

德美： 台灣好像到處都有吃吃喝喝的店。

老師： 對啊！中國人很重視吃，也很愛吃。

得中： 從我們一到台灣 就有朋友說要替我們接風。

歐福： 本來聽不懂，接風是什麼意思。

德美： 後來才知道，是請客吃飯，歡迎我們。

老師： 一邊吃飯一邊輕鬆聊天，氣氛就很好。

得中： 但是常常讓朋友花錢請客吃東西，很不好意思！

老師： 所以你也要找機會回請啊！

歐福： 可是我們是學生，沒有那麼多錢！

老師： 沒關係，重要的是心意。

得中： 心裡有這個意思就好了嗎？

老師： 不是！回請一杯他喜歡的飲料或是一塊小蛋糕就可
　　　　以了，如果是到朋友家做客，就帶一點水果，這樣就
　　　　是很好的答謝了，也不失禮。

	生詞	簡體字	詞類	拼音	英譯
1.	飽	饱	Adj.	bǎo	full
2.	小吃	小吃	N.	xiǎochī	snack(s)
3.	眼睛	眼睛	N.	yǎnjīng	eye(s)
4.	肚子	肚子	N.	dùzǐ	stomach
5.	夜市	夜市	N.	yèshì	night market
6.	嘴巴	嘴巴	N.	zuǐbā	lips, mouth
7.	改天	改天	N.	gǎitiān	some other time
8.	到處	到处	Adj.	dàochù	everywhere
9.	重視	重视	Adj.	zhòngshì	to consider important
10.	替	替	V.	tì	for, replace
11.	接風	接风	V./N.	jiēfēng	to welcome a guest from afar
12.	本來	本来	Adj.	běnlái	originally
13.	後來	后来	Adj.	hòulái	later on
14.	輕鬆	轻松	Adj.	qīngsōng	relax
15.	氣氛	气氛	N.	qìfēn	mood, atmosphere
16.	讓	让	V.	ràng	let, to yield
17.	回請	回请	V.	huí qǐng	to invite someone in return
18.	重要	重要	Adj.	zhòngyào	important
19.	心意	心意	N.	xīnyì	intention
20.	失禮	失礼	Adj.	shīlǐ	to be discourteous

【三‧生詞用法】

請填入適當的生詞

1. _____ 好好玩，有吃有喝又有得看。

2. 我們先吃_____了再出門吧！

3. 今天下雨，_____再去。

4. 我餓了，去夜市吃點_____吧！

5. 我沒帶眼鏡，_____很不舒服。

6. 老師很_____語法練習。

7. 台灣吃很方便，_____都是小吃店。

8. 我的_____太大，扣子扣不上了。

9. 他是一個大_____，你不要跟他說秘密。

10. 你看電腦看太久了，_____眼睛休息一下吧！

11. 替遠來的親友_____，就是請他們吃飯。

12. 上次是你請客，這次應該讓我_____你。

13. 人在國外，護照是最_____的東西。

14. 放_____一點，不要急慢慢來。

15. 我很喜歡這樣輕鬆的_____。

16. 我應該怎麼做，才不會_____？

17. 他本來是最慢的，沒想到他_____居上。

18. 她_____很生氣不說話，後來她就笑了。

19. 這是我們一點小小的_____，請你收下。

20. 我可以幫你，可是不能_____你做作業。

【四‧語法】

（1）…什麼…都/也…

問：再多吃一點，怎麼不吃了呢？

答：我什麼東西也吃不下了。

    1. 你去書店買了什麼書？   沒買
    2. 你跟老師說了什麼話？   沒說
    3. 你昨天去了什麼地方？   去了

（2）…來不及…

問：遊樂園好玩嗎？

答：太好玩了，我的眼睛都來不及看。

    1. 你怎麼寫那麼慢？   說得太快了／寫
    2. 你怎麼不吃早餐？   起得太晚了／吃
    3. 你怎麼沒告訴我？   決定得太晚了／告訴

（3）本來…，後來…

問：你本來要去哪裡？

答：我本來要去中國大陸，後來決定來台灣。

    1. 你不是今天沒事嗎？   沒事／忙死了
    2. 你不是只要一個包子嗎？   要一個／要了兩個
    3. 你不是要去逛街嗎？   去逛街／去看了電影

（4）讓…，真的…

問：本來說好一起去吃飯，為什麼又不去了呢？

答：每次都讓你們花那麼多錢，真的很不好意思。

    1. 要不要我去接你？   你來接我／太麻煩你了
    2. 我昨天很晚才回家。   父母擔心／是太不應該了
    3. 讓我來吧！   常常讓你幫忙／很不好意思

【五‧漢字】

1.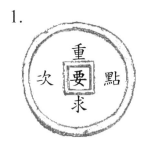
2.
3.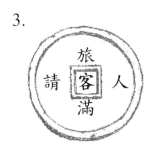

字⇨ 詞⇨ 句⇨ 文

1 要	重要	**重要**的事情先做。
	次要	重要的事情做完以後，再做**次要**的。
	要求	老師**要求**學生把字寫漂亮一點。
	要點	學生要求老師把考試的**要點**再說一次。

　　我們的老闆很好，每次開會說完**要點**就散會了，對員工的**要求**只有一個，**重要**的事情先做，**次要**的後做，自己分清楚就行了。

2 回	來回	**來回**票可以打九折。
	收回	說錯話可以**收回**嗎？
	回答	我不知道怎麼**回答**這個問題。
	回頭	「浪子**回頭**金不換」什麼意思？

　　你**回頭**看看是誰站在後面幫你？你為什麼不**回答**？
你媽媽每天**來來回回**，整理這些**回收**垃圾，賺一點小錢讓你唸書，你怎麼可以對你媽媽這樣說話？快跟她道歉**收回**那句話！　**回頭**是岸，知道錯了就好了！

3 客	旅客	各位**旅客**：請注意你們的隨身行李。
	請客	他一有錢就喜歡**請客**。
	客滿	這家餐廳天天**客滿**。
	客人	今天家裡有**客人**，我不能出去。

　　這家餐廳平常的生意就很好，經常**客滿**。我每次**請客**也都來這裡，**客人**都吃得很滿意。　今天人這麼多，大概是旅行團的**旅客**，我們去外面喝杯茶慢慢等吧！

【六．練習】

（1）

1. 我把重要的事情做完了，輕鬆地想飛。
2. 我吃得太飽了，什麼東西也吃不下了。
3. 別讓我吃不對的東西，我會肚子痛的。
4. 早餐吃得好，中餐吃得飽，晚餐吃得少。
5. 台灣很重視垃圾分類，可回收再利用就是資源。

（2）看圖說故事

蔡光輝

1. 中式西式都可以，我什麼都吃。
2. 讓我想想，來不及做大蛋糕，就做小的吧！
3. 你本來點的是小辣，我點的是大辣，後來都換成了中辣。
4. 先大火煮滾，然後中火煮十分鐘，最後再小火慢燉二十分鐘。
5. 我本來是吃樹葉的毛毛蟲，後來長大變成了蝴蝶，就吃花蜜。

（1）逛夜市
德美：好饱喔！我什么东西也吃不下了！
欧福：我很想试试所有的小吃，可是真的没办法了。
得中：我们的眼睛比我们的肚子大。
德美：夜市里吃的东西真的好多啊！
欧福：眼睛来不及看，嘴巴也来不及吃。
得中：老师也来不及说。
老师：没关系，改天再请小文带你们出来，慢慢看、慢慢吃。

（2）请客
德美：台湾好像到处都有吃吃喝喝的店。
老师：对啊！中国人很重视吃，也很爱吃。
得中：从我们一到台湾 就有朋友说要替我们接风。
欧福：本来听不懂，接风是什么意思。
德美：后来才知道，是请客吃饭，欢迎我们。
老师：一边吃饭一边轻松聊天，气氛就很好。
得中：但是常常让朋友花钱请客吃东西，很不好意思！
老师：所以你也要找机会回请啊！
欧福：可是我们是学生，没有那么多钱！
老师：没关系，重要的是心意。
得中：心里有这个意思就好了吗？
老师：不是！回请一杯他喜欢的饮料或是一块小蛋糕就可以
　　　了，如果是到朋友家做客，就带一点水果，
　　　这样就是很好的答谢了，也不失礼。

【八·拼音對照】

DÌ SĀN KÈ　　CHĪ HĒ WÉN HUÀ

（1）Guàng Yèshì
Déměi：　Hǎo bǎo o! Wǒ shéme dōngxi yě chī bú xià le!
Ōufú：　Wǒ hěn xiǎng shìshì suǒyǒu de xiǎochī, kěshì zhēnde
　　　　méi bànfǎ le.

Dézhōng: Wǒmen de yǎnjīng bǐ wǒmen de dùzi dà.

Déměi: Yěshì lǐ chī de dōngxi zhēnde hǎo duō a!

Ōufú: Yǎnjīng láibùjí kàn, zuǐbā yě láibùjí chī.

Dézhōng: Lǎoshī yě láibùjí shuō.

Lǎoshī: Méi guānxi, gǎitiān zài qǐng Xiǎowén dài nǐmen chūlái, mànmàn kàn, mànmàn chī.

(2) Qǐngkè

Déměi: Táiwān hǎoxiàng dàochù dōu yǒu chīchī hēhē de diàn.

Lǎoshī: Duì a! Zhōngguó rén hěn zhòngshì chī, yě hěn ài chī.

Dézhōng: Cóng wǒmen yí dào Táiwān, jiù yǒu péngyǒu shuō yào tì wǒmen jiēfēng.

Ōufú: Běnlái tīng bùdǒng, jiēfēng shì shéme yìsi.

Déměi: Hòulái cái zhīdào, shì qǐngkè chīfàn, huānyíng wǒmen.

Lǎoshī: Yìbiān chīfàn yìbiān qīngsōng liáotiān, qìfēn jiù hěn hǎo.

Dézhōng: Dànshì chángcháng ràng péngyǒu huā qián qǐngkè chī dōngxi, hěn bùhǎo yìsi!

Lǎoshī: Suǒyǐ nǐ yě yào zhǎo jīhuì huí qǐng a!

Ōufú: Kěshì wǒmen shì xuéshēng, méiyǒu nàme duō qián!

Lǎoshī: Méi guānxì, zhòngyào de shì xīnyì.

Dézhōng: Xīnlǐ yǒu nàge yìsi jiù hǎo le ma?

Lǎoshī: Búshì! Huíqǐng tā yìbēi tā xǐhuān de yǐnliào huòshì yíkuài xiǎo dàngāo jiù kěyǐ le, rúguǒ shì dào péngyǒu jiā zuòkè, jiù dài yìdiǎn shuǐguǒ, Zhèyàng jiùshì hěn hǎo de dáxiè le, yě bù shīlǐ.

【九 · 英文翻譯】

◆ **Dialogue** – p. 28~29

(1) Visiting the Night Market

Demei: I'm stuffed! I couldn't eat another thing!

Oufu: I'd really like to try all of the food, but there's really no way.

Dezhong: Our eyes are bigger than our stomachs.

Demei: There really are so many things to eat here in the night market!

Oufu: So much to see and so little time! So much to eat, and so little time!

Dezhong: Teacher also doesn't have enough time to explain it all to us.

Teacher: It doesn't matter, some other time Xiaowen can bring you here, and you can take your time looking around and enjoying the food.

(2) Treating

Demei: It looks like everywhere in Taiwan has places for eating and drinking.

Teacher: That's right! Chinese place a lot of importance on eating, and really love it.

Dezhong: Ever since coming to Taiwan, friends have been saying they wanted to treat us and make us feel welcome.

Oufu: Originally we didn't understand what "jie feng" meant.

Demei: Later we knew that it means to invite guests to dine, to welcome us.

Teacher: Leisurely eating and chatting makes for a pleasant atmosphere.

Dezhong: But it's really a little awkward and embarrassing to let friends spend so much money inviting us to eat so often!

Teacher: So, you need to find an opportunity to invite them out in return!

Oufu: But we're students and don't have that much money!

Teacher: That doesn't matter. It's the thought that counts.

Dezhong: So the important thing is that our intentions are good, and that's enough?

Teacher: No! You could treat your friends to a drink they like, or to have a piece of cake, for example. If you're invited to a friend's house, you should take along some fruit or something. This is a very good way to say "thank you", and is also courteous.

◆ **Vocabulary** – **p. 30~31**

1. night market Night markets are a lot of fun. There are things to eat and things to drink and things to see.

2.	full	After we eat our fill, then we can go out!
3.	some other time	It's raining today, so we'll go some other time.
4.	snack(s)	I'm hungry. Let's go to the night market and have some snacks.
5.	eyes	I didn't wear my glasses, so my eyes are very uncomfortable.
6.	to consider important	Teacher emphasizes grammar drills.
7.	everywhere	Eating in Taiwan is very convenient. There are little food shops everywhere!
8.	stomach	My stomach is too big. I can't button my buttons.
9.	lips, mouth	He is a blabbermouth. You don't want to tell him any secrets.
10.	let, to yield	You have been looking at the computer too long, and need to let your eyes rest awhile.
11.	to welcome a guest from afar	To welcome a visitor from afar, invite them to dine.
12.	to invite in return	Last time you paid, so this time it's my treat.
13.	important	While abroad, one's passport is the most important object.
14.	relax	Relax a little, don't rush, take your time!
15.	mood	I really like this relaxed atmosphere.
16.	to be discourteous	What should we do to avoid being discourteous?
17.	originally	Originally, he was the slowest. Surprisingly, he is now the first.
18.	later on	She was originally very angry with me and wouldn't talk. Later on, she was smiling.
19.	intention	This is a little something intended to show our gratitude. Please accept it.
20.	for	I can help you but I cannot do the homework for you.

◆ Grammar – p. 32

(1) Q: Do eat a little bit more!　Why have you stopped?
　　A: I couldn't eat another thing!
　1. What did you buy in the bookstore?　/ didn't buy
　2. What did you say to the teacher?　　/ didn't say
　3. Where did you go yesterday?　　　　/ went everywhere

(2) Q: Was that amusement park fun/interesting?
　　A: It was a lot of fun, but I didn't have time to see everything.
　1. How come you write so slowly?　　　　/ too fast
　2. Why didn't you eat your breakfast?　　/ too late
　3. Why didn't you tell me?　　　　　　　/ too late

(3) Q: Where did you originally want to go?
　　A: I originally wanted to go to China, but later decided to come to
　　　Taiwan.
　1. Weren't you free today?　　　　　　　/ extremely busy
　2. Didn't you only want one?　　　　　　/ wanted two
　3. Weren't you going to go window shopping?　/ went to a movie

(4) Q: Originally we'd agreed to go out to eat, so why didn't you go?
　　A: Letting you spend so much money every time really is embarrassing.
　1. Do you want me to pick you up?　/ too troublesome
　2. Did you go home very late?　　/ really shouldn't
　3. Let me help you!　　　ask you for help too often/ feel embarrassed

◆ Word to Sentence – p. 33

1 要	important, importance	The important thing is to take care of this business first.
	next in importance, second priority	After dealing with the most important business, then take care of the next thing on your list.

	require, demand	The teacher asks that students write their Chinese characters a little more beautifully.
	key points	The students ask that the teacher explain the key points of the test one more time.

Our boss is really great!   Every time we finish discussing the key points at a meeting, we can all leave!   The boss only asks one thing of the employees, "Take care of first things first, then deal with the next most important!", and we are left to decide for ourselves which is which.

2 回	round trip	A round trip ticket can get a ten percent discount.
	take back	When you say something wrong, can you take it back?
	reply, answer	I don't know how to answer your question.
	return, turn back, to turn one's head, to repent	"Langzi hui tou jin bu huan." means "The return of the prodigal is more precious than gold."

Have you ever looked back to see who has been helping you?   Why don't you answer?   Your mother has to travel back and forth every day, picking up recyclable items to make a little money so that you can study. How could you talk to your mother like that?   Apologize quickly and take back what you said.   Repent, and salvation is at hand!   Once you realize the error of your ways, everything will be all right.

3 客	passenger, traveler	Will all passengers please pay attention to their luggage?
	invite, treat	Whenever he has any money he likes to treat his friends.
	full of customers	This restaurant is always full of customers.
	guest	We have a guest at home today, so I can't go out.

This restaurant's business is usually pretty good, and is frequently full of customers.   Every time I invite guests to dine here, they are all very satisfied.   Today there are so many customers. Perhaps they're passengers from a tour group.   Let's go outside and drink some tea while we're waiting for a table.

第四課　我需要換台幣

【一‧對話】

（1）換台幣

德美： 老師，在台灣可以用美金或是歐元嗎？

老師： 只有大飯店才收外幣，你們有人需要換外幣嗎？

德美： 我需要，我要用歐元換台幣。

德中： 我也需要，我要用美金換台幣。

歐福： 我要用旅行支票換台幣。

老師： 好好好，都沒問題，都可以換。請你們帶著護照、
美金、歐元、旅行支票，跟我去銀行。

（2）在銀行

老師：　請你們每一個人填一張表。填上你們的姓名、出生年
　　　　月日、護照號碼、電話、地址、要換多少錢？

德美：　換錢為什麼要填寫我們的出生年月日？

老師：　我也不清楚，可能想知道你是不是未成年。奇怪？有
　　　　的銀行不會問這個問題。

德中：　老師，請問現在這個交換的價錢好不好？

老師：　你是說匯率嗎？還可以！要用多少，就換多少，不要
　　　　一次換太多，不佔便宜，也不吃虧。

歐福：　填好了，現在該做什麼？

老師：　填好了以後，就到號碼機那裡去拿一個號碼，等你的
　　　　號碼到了，就去那個櫃台換台幣。

　　　　（在銀行裡大家都換好了台幣）

德美：　你們看！老師無聊得睡著了！

德中：　老師，對不起，讓您久等了。謝謝您的幫忙！

歐福：　現在我們都是有錢人了，可以請你喝一杯飲料嗎？

	生詞	簡體字	詞類	拼音	英譯
1.	外幣	外币	N.	wàibì	foreign currency
2.	填表	填表	V.	tiánbiǎo	to fill in a form
3.	清楚	清楚	Adj.	qīngchǔ	clear
4.	成年	成年	Adj.	chéngnián	legally adult
5.	奇怪	奇怪	Adj.	qí guài	odd, strange, unusual
6.	護照	护照	N.	hù zhào	passport
7.	銀行	银行	N.	yínháng	bank
8.	交換	交换	V.	jiāohuàn	exchange
9.	價錢	价钱	N.	jiàqián	price
10.	匯率	汇率	N.	huìlǜ	exchange rate
11.	佔便宜	占便宜	V.	zhànpiányí	to take advantage
12.	吃虧	吃亏	V.	chīkuī	to endure a loss or disadvantage
13.	號碼機	号码机	N.	hàomǎjī	number machine
14.	櫃台	柜台	N.	guìtái	counter
15.	無聊	无聊	Adj.	wúliáo	bored, boring
16.	飲料	饮料	N.	yǐnliào	drink, beverage

【三‧生詞用法】

請填入適當的生詞

1. 你才十五歲，未_____的人不能喝酒。
2. 你得要先_____，再拿到那個櫃台去。
3. 我不集郵，我收集_____。
4. 請問_____幾點休息？
5. 這種表要填寫得很_____。
6. 你問的這個問題太_____了。
7. 我們可以做語言_____的同學嗎？
8. 你的_____快到期了，注意別讓它過期。
9. 這個_____不合理，不要買了。
10. _____的變動是一個大問題。
11. _____一點_____沒關係。
12. 有的_____會自動叫號碼。
13. 你在那個_____等了多久？
14. 等人是一件最_____的事情。
15. 請問你有無糖_____嗎？
16. 他老是想_____別人的_____。

【四．語法】

（1）只有…才…

問：請問哪裡收外幣？　答：只有大飯店才收外幣。

    1.請問哪裡有好吃的餐廳？　　　　當地人
    2.請問到你家要坐幾號公車？　　　開車
    3.哪裡有「愛」這本書？　　　　　圖書館

（2）帶著…，到…

問：我們需要帶什麼？
答：請你們帶著護照，到銀行辦理。

    1.請問要怎麼申請延長簽證？　　　資料／辦公室
    2.請問在哪裡繳費？　　　　　　　帳單／繳費處
    3.我要怎麼辦理借書證？　　　　　證件／圖書館

（3）每…

問：我們要填什麼？　答：每一個人填一張表。

    1.你上幾堂中文課？　　　　　　　一個星期
    2.公車多久來一班？　　　　　　　半個小時
    3.你上中文課有休息時間嗎？　　　一堂課

（4）要…，就…。不要…太多。

問：我們應該換多少錢？
答：要用多少，就換多少。不要一次換太多。

    1.這個週末要做什麼？　　　　　　做／想
    2.放假計畫去哪裡？　　　　　　　去／考慮
    3.你想請誰來喝喜酒？　　　　　　請／擔心

【五・漢字】

1.

2.

3.

字⇨ 詞⇨ 句⇨ 文

1 護	保護	媽媽**保護**孩子，孩子**保護**寵物。
	愛護	教孩子**愛護**花草、小動物。
	護照	**護照**是出國的時候最重要的東西。
	護士	那位**護士**常常陪病人聊天。

　　那家眼科醫院的醫生很好，經常教他的病人，怎麼**愛護**自己的眼睛。有一次我去看病，不小心把我的**護照**掉在醫院裡了，醫生請護士打電話給我，要我快去拿，他說**護照**是人在國外最重要的東西，要好好**保護**它。

2 聊	無聊	**無聊**的時候就上網找網友聊天。
	閒聊	他們一天到晚**閒聊**別人的事，真無聊。
	聊天	老人家沒事做，就喜歡找人**聊天**。
	聊聊	**聊聊**家人、聊聊孩子，時間過得好快。

　　她**無聊**的時候喜歡找人**聊天**，聊家人的健康、聊孩子的工作、聊最近的生活。東**聊聊**西**聊聊**，很難說這是關心還是多事！總之，她生活得很開心，沒事**閒聊**也是一種交際，不要去**聊**別人的閒事就好了。

3 虧	幸虧	**幸虧**我多帶了錢，要不然就麻煩了！
	吃虧	**吃虧**可以學得經驗，反而得到好處。
	虧錢	生意人不可能做**虧錢**的生意。
	虧本	我如果便宜賣給你，我就**虧本**了！

　　做生意有時候賺錢，有時候**虧錢**，這是很正常的。這次**幸虧**我把本錢先存起來了，要不然就要**吃大虧**了。吃一點小虧，**虧了小錢**還好，**虧了本錢**就糟糕了。

【六 · 練習】

(1) 魔鏡

上中蜜領路
台國心蜂帶線
上中中蜜領路

1. 　　　　　　　他一**上台**就忘了要說什麼！
2. 　　　　　妳昨天在**台上**的表現很好。
3. 　你現在在亞洲，就應該去**中國**大陸看看。
4. 　　　　台灣的**國中**教育是三年。
5. 　　　　住在市**中心**，交通比較方便。
6. 　　　應該把**心中**的感謝跟愛說出來。
7. 　學生跟著老師的**帶領**，安全下山。
8. 這麼熱的天氣，打**領帶**真不合適。
9. 　　　　　　**蜜蜂**忙著採花蜜。
10. 　檸檬茶加一點**蜂蜜**，味道好極了！
11. 　你確定走這條**路線**是對的嗎？
12. 電話**線路**跟網路**線路**是連線的嗎？

(2) 看圖說故事

蔡光輝

1. 想坐小火車，只有阿里山才有。
2. 我們各付各的，誰都不佔便宜不吃虧。
3. 每到週末，帶著書到郊外走走，要休息就休息，不要想太多。
4. 我用這根香蕉跟你換那顆花生，你一定不吃虧。
5. 先有雞或是先有蛋？這個問題誰也不清楚。

（1）换台币

德美： 老师，在台湾可以用美金或是欧元吗？

老师： 只有大饭店才收外币，你们有人需要换外币吗？

德美： 我需要，我要用欧元换台币。

德中： 我也需要，我要用美金换台币。

欧福： 我要用旅行支票换台币。

老师： 好好好，都没问题，都可以换。请你们带着护照、美金、欧元、旅行支票，跟我去银行。

（2）在银行

老师： 请你们每一个人填一张表。填上你们的姓名、出生年月日、护照号码、电话、地址、要换多少钱？

德美： 换钱为什么要填写我们的出生年月日？

老师： 我也不清楚，可能想知道你是不是未成年。奇怪？有的银行不会问这个问题。

德中： 老师，请问现在这个交换的价钱好不好？

老师： 你是说汇率吗？还可以！要用多少，就换多少，不要一次换太多，不占便宜，也不吃亏。

欧福： 填好了，现在该做什么？

老师： 填好了以后，就到号码机那里去拿一个号码，等你的号码到了，就去那个柜台换台币。（在银行里大家都换好了台币）

德美： 你们看！老师无聊得睡着了！

德中： 老师，对不起，让您久等了。谢谢您的帮忙！

欧福： 现在我们都是有钱人了，可以请你喝一杯饮料吗？

【八·拼音對照】

DÌ SÌ KÈ　　WǑ XŪYÀO HUÀN TÁIBÌ

（1） Huàn Táibì

Déměi: Lǎoshī, zài Táiwān, kěyǐ yòng Měijīn huòshì Ōuyuán ma?

Lǎoshī: Zhǐyǒu dà fàndiàn cái shōu wàibì, nǐmen yǒu rén xūyào huàn wàibì ma?

Déměi: Wǒ xūyào, wǒ yào yòng Ōuyuán huàn Táibì.

Dézhōng: Wǒ yě xūyào, wǒ yào yòng Měijīn huàn Táibì.

Ōufú: Wǒ yào yòng lǚxíng zhīpiào huàn Táibì.

Lǎoshī : Hǎo hǎo hǎo, dōu méi wèntí, dōu kěyǐ huàn. Qǐng nǐmen dàizhe hùzhào, Měijīn, Ōuyuán, lǚxíng zhīpiào, gēn wǒ qù yínháng.

(2) Zài Yínháng

Lǎoshī: Qǐng nǐmen měi yíge rén tián yìzhāng biǎo.Tián shàng nǐmen de xìngmíng, chūshēng nián yuè rì, hùzhào hàomǎ, diànhuà, dìzhǐ, yào huàn duōshǎo qián?

Déměi: Huàn qián wèishéme yào tiánxiě wǒmen de chūshēng nián yuè rì?

Lǎoshī: Wǒ yě bù qīngchǔ, kěnéng xiǎng zhīdào nǐ shì búshì wèi chéngnián. Qíguài?yǒude yínháng búhuì wèn zhèige wèntí.

Dézhōng: Lǎoshī, qǐngwèn xiànzài zhèige jiāohuàn de jiàqián hǎo bùhǎo?

Lǎoshī: Nǐ shì shuō huìlǜ ma? Hái kěyǐ! Yào yòng duōshǎo, jiù huàn duōshǎo, búyào yícì huàn tàiduō, bú zhàn piányí, yě bù chīkuī.

Ōufú: Tián hǎo le, xiànzài gāi zuò shéme?

Lǎoshī: Tián hǎo le yǐhòu, jiù dào hàomǎjī nàlǐ qù ná yíge hàomǎ, děng nǐde hàomǎ dào le, jiù qù nèige guìtái huàn Táibì. (Zài yínháng lǐ dàjiā dōu huàn hǎo le táibì.)

Déměi: Nǐmen kàn! Lǎoshī wúliáo de shuìzháo le!

Dézhōng: Lǎoshī, duìbùqǐ, ràng nín jiǔděng le. Xièxie nín de bāngmáng!

Ōufú: Xiànzài wǒmen dōu shì yǒu qián rén le,kěyǐ qǐng nǐ hē yìbēi yǐnliào ma?

◆ Dialogue – p. 42~43

(1) Exchanging NT Dollars

Demei: Teacher, can I use American dollars or Euros in Taiwan?

Teacher: Only big hotels will accept foreign currency. Do any of you need to change your money to NT dollars?

Demei: I do. I need to change Euros for NT dollars.

Dezhong: I do, too. I need to exchange American dollars for NT dollars.

Oufu: I need to cash my traveler's checks.

Teacher: Okay, okay! No problem! We can change all your currency. Please bring your American dollars, Euros, traveler's checks and passports, and come with me to the bank.

(2) At the Bank

Teacher: Will each of you please fill in a form? Write your name, date of birth, passport number, telephone number and address, and how much money you want to exchange.

Demei: Why do we need to fill in our birthdays?

Teacher: I'm not clear about that, either. Maybe they want to know if you are underage. That's very strange - some banks will not ask this question.

Dezhong: Teacher, is right now a good price to change?

Teacher: Do you mean the exchange rate? It's okay. Just exchange whatever you need, do not exchange too much. That way, you won't lose or gain too much as the rates change.

Oufu: My form is filled in. Now what do I do?

Teacher: After you fill out the form, go to take a number, wait for your turn, and go to the counter.

            (After everyone has finished exchanging their money.)

Demei: Hey, look! Teacher has fallen asleep due to boredom.

Dezhong: I'm sorry we kept you waiting. Thank you for your help, Teacher.

Oufu: We are all rich now! Can we buy you something to drink?

◆ Vocabulary – p. 45

1.	legally adult, mature	You are only fifteen. You are too young to drink alcohol.
2.	to fill in a form	First, you need to fill in the form, then take it to that counter.
3.	foreign currency	I don't collect stamps. I collect foreign currency.
4.	bank	Excuse me, what time does the bank close?
5.	clear	This kind of form needs to be filled in very clearly.
6.	odd, strange, unusual	This question is too strange!
7.	exchange	Can we be language exchange partners?
8.	passport	Your passport will need to be renewed soon. Pay attention and don't let it expire!
9.	price	This price is not reasonable. Don't buy it!
10.	exchange rate	Fluctuating exchange rates are a big problem.
11.	to endure a loss or disadvantage	A disadvantage doesn't matter.
12.	number machine	Some of the number machines will automatically call your number.
13.	counter	How long have you been waiting at that counter?
14.	bored, boring	Waiting for someone is so boring!
15.	drink, beverage	Excuse me, do you have any sugar free drinks?
16.	to take advantage	He is always looking out to gain an advantage over others.

◆ Grammar – p. 46

(1) Q: Excuse me, which places can accept foreign currency?
   A: Only large hotels will accept foreign currency.
   1. Where are the best restaurants?   / local people
   2. Which bus route goes to your house?   / drive
   3. Where is the book LOVE?   / the library

(2) Q: What do we need to bring?

  A: Please bring your passports and take care of this business in the
   bank.

  1. How do we apply for a visa extension?   / information
  2. Where should I pay?   / bill
  3. How can I apply for a library card?   / identity card

(3) Q: What do we need to fill in?   **A:** Each person must fill in one form.
  1. How many Chinese lessons do you take?   / each week
  2. How often does the bus come?   / every half hour
  3. Is there a break between classes?   / every session

(4) Q: How much money should we exchange?

  A: Exchange whatever you need.   Do not exchange too much.
  1. What do you want to do this weekend?   / whatever you want
  2. What are your plans for the vacation?   / wherever you want to go
  3. Who do you want to invite to the banquet? / whoever you want to invite

◆ Word to Sentence – p. 47

1 護	protect, take care of	Mothers take care of children, and children take care of their pets.
	cherish	Teach children to cherish plants, flowers and small animals.
	passport	A passport is the most important thing to have when you go abroad.
	nurse	That nurse often chats with patients.

The doctor at that ophthalmology hospital is very good. He always teaches his patients how to cherish and protect their eyesight. Once, when I went there for an examination, I carelessly left my passport at the hospital. The doctor asked the nurse to give me a call to come back quickly to pick it up. He said, "A passport is the most important thing for a person traveling abroad, and it must be carefully taken care of."

2 聊	bored, boring	When you're feeling bored, just get on the Internet and chat with friends.
	gossip, chat	They sit around chatting and gossiping all day! It's so boring!
	chat	When older people don't have anything to do, they like to find someone to talk with.
	leisurely discuss	Time passes so quickly while leisurely discussing family and children!

When she's bored, she enjoys finding someone to chat with, discussing her family's health, the children's work, and recent events in her life. Discussing this, that and the other, it's hard to tell if she is expressing concern or just being nosey! Well anyway, her life is a pretty happy one, and if she has nothing else to do, chatting about things is one kind of social function. As long as one doesn't gossip about others, that's okay.

3 虧	fortunately	Fortunately I've got enough money on me! Otherwise there would've been a problem!
	bad experience, to be placed at a disadvantage	One can learn from bad experiences and setbacks, and turn something negative into something positive.
	lose money	Businessmen will not get involved in a money-losing deal.
	to suffer a deficit	If I were to sell it to you more cheaply, I would not break even on this deal!

When doing business, sometimes you make money and sometimes you lose money. That's just normal. This time, fortunately I'd saved the capital, otherwise I would have been put at a serious disadvantage. Having a minor setback, or losing a little money is all right, but losing all of one's capital would be a disaster!

閱讀 （一）

　　這是我第一次來台灣，高雄人就像南台灣的太陽一樣熱情。

　　我一下飛機，我的台灣女朋友就來機場接我。我和阿玉是在英國認識的，她是我的同學，也是我的中文老師。我打算在高雄待一個星期，住在阿玉家，然後再和阿玉一起回英國。我們先去銀行換台幣，就到阿玉家去吃飯了。跟阿玉的家人見面，我非常緊張。阿玉叫我放輕鬆，如果聽不懂中文，什麼都不用說，微笑、點頭就好了。

　　阿玉的父母很親切，弟弟妹妹很愛說話。自我介紹完了以後，就開始吃飯。阿玉的父母說的中文我聽不懂，我就一直微笑、點頭，<u>碗裡的菜越來越多</u>，他們一直說「吃，吃，吃」。阿玉的爸爸拿了兩瓶台灣啤酒，叫我「乾，乾，乾」。如果我沒喝完杯子裡的酒，她爸爸就不高興。好不容易，晚餐結束了。她爸爸打開電視，拿出麥克風，弟弟妹妹開始一邊看電視，一邊唱歌，這就是卡拉 OK。

　　來台灣的第一個晚上就讓我感覺到高雄的熱情。不知道明天高雄的太陽怎麼樣？

1. 作者和阿玉是什麼關係？
2. 如果聽不懂中文該怎麼辦？
3. 為什麼作者<u>碗裡的菜越來越多</u>？
4. 阿玉的爸爸說「乾，乾，乾」，是什麼意思？

複習 （一）

一、填空

1. 大家好！我給你們_____一下，在我旁邊的這兩位是_____德國來的同學。

2. 嗨！好久不見！妳_____來_____漂亮了！

3. 我們_____今天要去爬山，_____因為下雨所以取消了。

4. 星期天，_____你來幫我搬家，真的不好意思。

5. 這是現磨的咖啡，你要喝_____，就煮_____，不要一次煮太多，要喝再煮。

6. 你要的書，只有學校附近的書店_____有。

二、連連看

（ a ） 例： 大家好，我是金貝山

（　） 1. 台灣到處都有吃吃喝喝的店，每天吃一家都行，

（　） 2. 他來台灣才半年，

（　） 3. 小王常請我吃飯，真不好意思，

（　） 4. 你上課來不及了，

（　） 5. 他為什麼要你的護照，我也不清楚，

　　　 a. 你們可以叫我阿山。

　　　 b. 有機會我一定要回請他。

　　　 c. 可能想知道你是不是未成年吧。

　　　 d. 但是常常這樣，身體會受不了。

　　　 e. 不但中文說得好，台灣話也會說了。

　　　 f. 我看你還是坐計程車去吧！

第五課　遊山玩水

【一‧對話】

（1）旅行

歐福：　這是我們第一次到台灣來，
　　　　請你們介紹一下哪裡好玩。

小文：　當然最好能環島旅行。

阿山：　對！從南玩到北，
　　　　再從北往東走。

老師：　這是一個好建議。

阿山：　台灣東部的山很美，一邊是山，一邊是海。

德美：　我聽說台灣東部的風景非常漂亮！

得中：　我看過簡介，那裡還有原住民對不對？

小文：　對對對！阿山就是從台東來的原住民，
　　　　他可以做導遊。

阿山：　沒問題！到台東找我，我是土生土長的台東人！

(2) 怎麼去？

德美： 怎麼去比較好呢？

小文： 台灣的火車很舒服，環島的觀光票也不貴。

歐福： 我們可以租車嗎？

得中： 我也覺得自己開車比較自由，可以租車環島。

老師： <u>自由是自由，可是你們剛來台灣</u>……

得中： 老師怕我們<u>對台灣的情形不熟</u>。

歐福： 我們可以看地圖。

老師： 不是怕你們迷路，是怕開車人的習慣不同。

德美： 我們就聽老師的建議，<u>還是坐火車比較安全</u>。

【二・生詞】

	生詞	簡體字	詞類	拼音	英譯
1.	當然	当然	Adv.	dāngrán	of course
2.	環島	环岛	V./N.	huándǎo	to travel around the island
3.	旅行	旅行	V.	lǚxíng	traveling
4.	建議	建议	N.	jiànyì	suggestion, advice, recommendation
5.	聽說	听说	V.	tīngshuō	to have heard
6.	風景	风景	N.	fēngjǐng	scenery, scenic spots
7.	簡介	简介	N.	jiǎnjiè	brochure; introduction
8.	原住民	原住民	N.	yuánzhùmín	aborigine(s)
9.	導遊	导游	N.	dǎoyóu	tour guide
10.	土生土長	土生土长	Adj.	tǔ shēng tǔ zhǎng	to be born and raised in a certain place
11.	舒服	舒服	Adj.	shūfú	comfortable
12.	租車	租车	V.	zū chē	to rent a car
13.	自由	自由	Adj.	zìyóu	free, freedom
14.	怕	怕	V.	pà	to fear, be afraid, worried
15.	情形	情形	N.	qíngxíng	situation, condition
16.	熟	熟	Adj.	shóu	to be familiar with
17.	地圖	地图	N.	dìtú	map
18.	迷路	迷路	V.	mílù	to be lost
19.	習慣	习惯	N.	xíguàn	used to, accustomed to, custom, habit
20.	安全	安全	Adj.	ānquán	safe, safety

請填入適當的生詞

1. 請問你有這裡的＿＿＿＿＿嗎？我們想多認識認識這裡。
2. 去國外旅行，可以看各地不一樣的＿＿＿＿＿。
3. 旅行社說這是去國外＿＿＿＿＿最好的時候。
4. 我的夢想是先＿＿＿＿＿再環遊世界。
5. 我很想去看看＿＿＿＿＿的保留區。
6. ＿＿＿＿＿你要出國了，是真的嗎？
7. 你需要我幫忙，我＿＿＿＿＿願意幫你。
8. ＿＿＿＿＿的工作很有意思，可是很累。
9. 不知道該怎麼辦，就應該多聽聽別人的＿＿＿＿＿。
10. 我對這裡不熟，你可以畫一張＿＿＿＿＿給我嗎？
11. 我們在這裡人生地不＿＿＿＿＿，怎麼辦？
12. 如果你＿＿＿＿＿了，就打電話給我。
13. 我們都是＿＿＿＿＿的台灣人。
14. ＿＿＿＿＿比坐車貴多了。
15. 有我在，＿＿＿＿＿什麼？
16. 這個時候的天氣真＿＿＿＿＿！不冷也不熱。
17. 我就是怕會有這種＿＿＿＿＿，所以才不同意的。
18. 一個人晚上出去，不＿＿＿＿＿，容易遇到壞人。
19. 為什麼不讓他說話？每個人都有說話的＿＿＿＿＿。
20. 剛到台灣的時候，常吃不好，後來＿＿＿＿＿就好了！

（1）從…到…

問：請問你們什麼時候開門？
答：從早上十點開到晚上十點。

1. 洗手間怎麼走？　　　　這裡／到底，在右邊
2. 開車到台南要多久？　　高雄／台南，差不多半個小時
3. 你上班的時間是…？　　早上八點／下午五點

（2）…是…，可是…

問：怎麼了？你不喜歡吃嗎？
答：喜歡是喜歡，可是太油了。

1. …不好嗎？　　好／太多了
2. …不夠大嗎？　大／太長了
3. …不方便嗎？　方便／太吵了

（3）對…不熟

問：你去過法國嗎？　答：去過，可是我對法國不熟。

1. 認識…嗎？
2. 知道…嗎？
3. 會用…嗎？

（4）還是…比較…

問：你覺得租車怎麼樣？　答：我覺得還是坐火車比較好。

1. 吃中飯／吃晚飯
2. 換一千塊／換五百塊
3. 紅色／綠色

【五‧漢字】

1.

2.

3.

字⇨ 詞⇨ 句⇨ 文

1 認	否認	那個小偷承認偷車，但是**否認**殺人。
	承認	我**承認**錯了，請你原諒我。
	認真	學生**認真**上課，是老師最高興的事了！
	認為	你**認為**他們兩個人是認真的嗎？

　　如果你**認為**我跟他快要結婚了，那你就錯了。我**承認**我們兩個人都很**認真**，但是我**否認**「快要結婚」的這種消息。

2 遊	郊遊	春天很適合到郊外去**郊遊**、野餐。
	導遊	我們**導遊**的知識很豐富。
	遊記	我從出發的第一天就開始寫**遊記**了。
	遊戲	不論大人、小孩都愛玩這種**遊戲**。

　　導遊說：出國旅遊跟當天來回的**郊遊**很不一樣，**郊遊**可以帶吃的、喝的，玩**遊戲**用的東西，你想帶多少東西都可以。可是旅遊就不一樣了，帶的行李越少越好，一台相機、一本本子，一枝筆寫**遊記**就夠了。

3 自	親自	你得要**親自**到銀行去開戶。
	私自	團體旅遊就不能**私自**行動。
	自助	這是**自助**式的，沒有服務員。
	自私	你讓整個團體等你一個人，真是太**自私**了！

　　這是我們幾個好朋友**私自**邀約的團體旅遊，不是對外公開的，所以旅費比較便宜。有些事你得**親自**動手做，也不能很**自私**的只管你自己，除了**自助**以外，還要助人。

【六・練習】

（1）魔鏡

茶出出實人人　點生租現工情　茶出出實人人　點生租現工情

（2）賓果遊戲

這附近	我的夢想	是他	請來的	工人
有房子	點茶的客人	已經	生出來的	常常有
出租嗎	租出去了	要換	實現了	好點子
現在	人工貴	出生證明	茶點	人情
現實一點	撿到一百萬	是不可能的	夢中情人	不見了

(3) 看圖說故事 － 停看聽

1. 借酒裝瘋
   喝多了，話就會多。
   話多了，就會討人厭。
   討人厭了，麻煩就來了！

2. 避之大吉
   聽到麻煩，假裝沒聽到。
   看到麻煩，假裝沒看到。
   沒你的事，趕快走開！

3. 無理取鬧
   碰到不講理的人，
   碰到不合理的事，
   二話不說，快打電話！

（1）旅行

欧福：　这是我们第一次到台湾来，请你们介绍一下哪里好玩。

小文：　当然最好能环岛旅行。

阿山：　对！从南玩到北，再从北往东走。

老师：　这是一个好建议。

阿山：　台湾东部的山很美，一边是山，一边是海。

德美：　我听说台湾东部的风景非常漂亮！

得中：　我看过简介，那里还有原住民对不对？

小文：　对对对！阿山就是从台东来的原住民，他可以做导游。

阿山：　没问题！到台东找我，我是土生土长的台东人！

（2）怎么去？

德美：　怎么去比较好呢？

小文：　台湾的火车很舒服，环岛的观光票也不贵。

欧福：　我们可以租车吗？

得中：　我也觉得自己开车比较自由，可以租车环岛。

老师：　自由是自由，可是你们刚来台湾……

得中：　老师怕我们对台湾的情形不熟。

欧福：　我们可以看地图。

老师：　不是怕你们迷路，是怕开车人的习惯不同。

德美：　我们就听老师的建议，还是坐火车比较安全。

【八·拼音對照】

DÌ WǓ KÈ　　YÓU SHĀN WÁN SHUǏ

（1）Lǚxíng

Ōufú:　　Zhèshì wǒmen dì yī cì dào Táiwān lái, qǐng nǐmen jièshào yí xià nǎlǐ hǎo wán.

Xiǎowén:　Dāngrán zuì hǎo néng huándǎo lǚxíng.

Āshān:　　Duì! Cóng nán wán dào běi, zài cóng běi wǎng dōng zǒu.

Lǎoshī: Zhèshì yíge hǎo jiànyì.

Āshān: Táiwān dōngbù de shān hěn měi, yìbiān shì shān, yìbiān shì hǎi.

Déměi: Wǒ tīngshuō Táiwān dōngbù de fēngjǐng fēicháng piàoliàng!

Dézhōng: Wǒ kàn guò jiǎnjiè, nàlǐ hái yǒu yuánzhùmín duì búduì?

Xiǎowén: Duì duì duì! Āshān jiùshì Táidōng lái de yuánzhùmín, tā kěyǐ zuò dǎoyóu.

Āshān: Méi wèntí! Dào Táidōng zhǎo wǒ, wǒ shì tǔ shēng tǔ zhǎng de Táidōng rén!

(2) Zěnme Qù

Déměi: Zěnme qù bǐjiào hǎo ne?

Xiǎowén: Táiwān de huǒchē hěn shūfú, huándǎo de guānguāng piào yě bú guì.

Ōufú: Wǒmen kěyǐ zū chē ma?

Dézhōng: Wǒ yě juéde zìjǐ kāichē bǐjiào zìyóu, kěyǐ zūchē huándǎo.

Lǎoshī: Zìyóu shì zìyóu, kěshì nǐmen gāng lái Táiwān…

Dézhōng: Lǎoshī pà wǒmen duì Táiwān de qíngxíng bù shóu.

Ōufú: Wǒmen kěyǐ kàn dìtú.

Lǎoshī: Búshì pà nǐmen mílù, shì pà kāichē de rén xíguàn bùtóng.

Déměi: Wǒmen jiù tīng Lǎoshī de jiànyì, háishì zuò huǒchē bǐjiào ānquán.

【九 · 英文翻譯】

◆ **Dialogue** – p. 58~59

(1) Traveling

Oufu: This is our first time in Taiwan. Could you please recommend some interesting places to visit?

Xiaowen: It would be great if you could travel around the island.

Ashan:	Right! Travel from south to north, and again from the north to the east.
Teacher:	This is a very good suggestion.
Ashan:	The mountains on the east coast of Taiwan are very beautiful, with mountains on one side and the ocean on the other.
Demei:	I have heard that the scenery on the east coast is very beautiful!
Dezhong:	I've seen a travel brochure that said there are still aborigines. Is that true?
Xiaowen:	Yes, that's right! Ashan is an aborigine from Taidong, so he could be the guide.
Ashan:	No problem! When you come to Taidong, look me up. I was born and raised in Taidong!

(2) How to Get There

Demei:	What's the best way to get there?
Xiaowen:	Taiwan's trains are very comfortable, and tickets for touring around the island aren't expensive.
Oufu:	Couldn't we rent a car?
Dezhong:	I feel like driving a car would give us more freedom, too. We could rent one to drive around the island.
Teacher:	Freedom is all very well and good, but you've only just arrived in Taiwan….
Dezhong:	Are you worried that we might not be familiar with Taiwan?
Oufu:	We can look at a map.
Teacher:	I'm not afraid you'll get lost, I'm just concerned about different driving habits.
Demei:	Well, let's listen to Teacher's advice. It's still safer to ride on the train.

◆ Vocabulary – p. 60~61

| 1. brochure | Excuse me, do you have this place's brochure? We would like to know this place better. |
| 2. scenery, scenic spots | While traveling abroad, one can see every place's different kinds of scenery. |

3.	traveling	The travel agency says this is the best time to travel abroad.
4.	travel around the island	My dream is to travel around the island first, and then to travel around the world.
5.	aborigine(s)	I would really like to see an aboriginal area.
6.	to have heard	I've heard you're going abroad. Is it true?
7.	of course	If you need my help, of course I'd be glad to help you.
8.	tour guide	Working as a tour guide is very interesting, but it's also very tiring.
9.	suggestion, advice, recommendation	If you don't know what to do, you should listen to others' advice.
10.	map	I'm not very familiar with this place. Could you draw me a map?
11.	to be familiar with	We are not familiar with the people and the place here. What should we do?
12.	to be lost	If you get lost, just give me a call.
13.	to be born and raised in a certain place	We are all born and raised in Taiwan.
14.	to rent a car	Renting a car is more expensive than riding a bus.
15.	to fear, be afraid, worried	If I'm here, what's there to be afraid of?
16.	comfortable	The weather right now is really very comfortable – not too cold and not too hot.
17.	situation, condition	I didn't agree because I was afraid this kind of situation would occur.
18.	safe, safety	It's not safe for one person to go out after dark, because it would be too easy to meet with a bad person.
19.	free, freedom	Why don't you let him talk? Everybody has the right to speak.
20.	used to, accustomed to, custom, habit	When I first arrived in Taiwan, I wasn't accustomed to the food, but after getting used to it, I'm fine now.

◆ Grammar – p. 62

(1) Q: Excuse me, when are you open for business?

A: We're open from ten a.m. to ten p.m.

1. Where is the bathroom?   Here / to the bottom, on the right
2. How long does it take to go to Tainan?
   Kaohsiung / Tainan, about half an hour
3. Working hours are…?
   Eight o'clock in the morning / five o'clock in the afternoon

(2) Q: What's up? Don't you like eating that?

A: It's all right, but it's too oily.

1. …not good?   All right, (but) too much
2. …not big enough?   It's big enough, but it's too long
3. …not convenient?   It's convenient, but it's too noisy

(3) Q: Have you been to France?

A: Yes, I have, but I'm not familiar with it.

1. Do you recognize…? / Do you know…?
2. Do you know…?
3. Do you know how to use…?

(4) Q: What do you think about renting a car?

A: I feel that riding a train would be better.

1. Eat lunch / eat supper
2. Get change for NT$1000 / get change for NT$500
3. Red / green

◆ Word to Sentence – p. 63

1 認	deny, refute	The thief confessed to stealing the car, but denied having murdered anyone.
	admit, confess	I admit that I was wrong. Please forgive me.
	diligent, serious	Diligent students are a teacher's greatest happiness!

	to think, consider	Do you think those two are serious about each other?

If you think I'm marrying him soon, you're mistaken.　I do admit that we're "serious", but deny the news that we're getting married soon.

2 遊	to travel in the countryside	Spring is highly suitable for walks in the country and picnics.
	tour guide	Our tour guide is very knowledgeable.
	travel log	From the very first day of my trip, I started keeping this diary.
	game	It doesn't matter if you're young or old, everyone likes this game.

The tour guide says, "Traveling abroad is completely different from a one day trip to the countryside.　When taking a trip to the country, you can carry your own food and drinks, and bring along any games you might want to play.　You can bring whatever you like.　However, touring is different.　The less baggage you carry, the better – one camera, one notebook and one pen for writing your travel diary are enough."

3 自	personally, in person	You must go to the bank in person to open an account.
	privately, on one's own initiative	When traveling with a tour group, you aren't able to act on your own initiative.
	self-help, self-serve	This is a self-serve place, with no service staff.
	selfish, self-centered	You kept the entire tour group waiting just for you! You are really too selfish!

This tour group is made up of several good friends who have privately gotten together to travel, and is not open to outsiders.　Consequently, the travel expenses are relatively inexpensive.　Some things you will have to take care of personally, and you cannot selfishly think only of yourself. In addition to helping yourself, you will also have to help other members of the group.

◆ Practice

（2）**Bingo** p. 64

Make complete sentences by connecting the squares in their proper order. You may use three to five squares, which can be vertical, horizontal, or diagonal.

1. The customer who ordered the tea wants to change the snacks.
2. It's impossible to change one's birth certificate.
3. He is the one who offered the good idea.
4. Are there any houses for rent nearby?
5. (The house is) already rented out.
6. My dream has already come true.
7. Get real!   Finding a million dollars is impossible!
8. Nowadays, labor is very expensive.
9. He is the one who hired the laborers.
10. There's not much friendly feeling left.
11. "Prince Charming" has left the building!

（3）**Picture Story** p. 65

After practicing this exercise, cover the words and see if you can repeat the sentences just looking at the picture.

1. Using Inebriation as an Excuse
2. Avoiding Trouble is Good Luck
3. To Make Trouble without a Good Reason

第六課　接待家庭

【一‧對話】

(1) 在學校

得中：嗨！德美、歐福，這個週末我的接待家庭要帶我去墾丁，你們要不要一起去？

德美：那麼多人，方便嗎？

歐福：你問過你的接待家人沒有？

得中：還沒有，可是他家有一部九人座的休旅車，可以坐九個人。

歐福：<u>不是車子大小的問題，是禮貌上的問題。</u>

德美：你最好先問問你的家人，如果可以，我們當然求之不得！

得中：對不起！我真不懂事，我應該先問他們，再問你們的。

（2）好消息！

德美： 老師，剛才得中告訴我們一個好消息！

老師： 什麼好消息？

得中： 我的接待家庭要帶我們三個去墾丁玩！

老師： 那太好了！你們一定會玩得很開心！

歐福： 現在的油價那麼高，我們應該付油錢，對不對？

老師： 禮貌上先問一下，可是我想他們不會收。

德美： 那我們應該做什麼？

得中： 我知道，我們可以買一點吃的、喝的，或是水果。

歐福： 或是做幾個德國口味的三明治。

老師： 你們真懂事，你們的接待家人一定愛死你們了！

【二·生詞】

	生詞	簡體字	詞類	拼音	英譯
1.	週末	周末	N.	zhōumò	weekend
2.	接待	接待	V.	jiēdài	receive, greet, treat
3.	家庭	家庭	N.	jiātíng	family
4.	帶	帶	V.	dài	bring, take, carry
5.	墾丁	垦丁	N.	Kěndīng	Kenting
6.	座位	座位	N.	zuòwèi	seat
7.	休旅車	休旅车	N.	xiūlǚ chē	van
8.	禮貌	礼貌	Adj.	lǐmào	polite, courtesy
9.	求之不得	求之不得	I. E.	qiú zhī bù dé	to be exactly what one wanted
10.	懂事	懂事	Adj.	dǒngshì	to understand worldly affairs
11.	消息	消息	N.	xiāoxí	news, information
12.	開心	开心	V.	kāixīn	happy
13.	油價	油价	N.	yóu jià	gas price(s)
14.	油錢	油钱	N.	yóu qián	gas money
15.	口味	口味	N.	kǒuwèi	flavor, taste
16.	三明治	三明治	N.	sānmíngzhì	sandwich
17.	愛死	爱死	V.	ài sǐ	to love (someone or something) "to death"

【三・生詞用法】

填入適當的生詞

1. 我的_____很簡單，只有四個人。

2. 主人總是很熱情地_____客人。

3. 你要_____孩子去哪裡玩？

4. _____ 在台灣的南部。

5. 開_____去旅行很方便。

6. 對每個人都要有_____，才會受人喜愛。

7. 這個_____我有空，要不要出去玩？

8. 這個_____不太舒服，我們換一下吧！

9. 小孩子不_____，你不要生孩子的氣。

10. 我_____那隻小狗了！牠真的很可愛。

11. 我喜歡試試各種不同_____的蛋糕。

12. 你能這麼想，我就很_____了。

13. 最近的_____一天比一天高。

14. 這樣的_____，為什麼不早說？

15. 這個_____裡面夾了什麼？真好吃！

16. 我的飯錢都不夠了，當然更沒有_____了。

17. 這是我們_____的事情，怎麼會不答應呢？

【四‧語法】

(1) …過…沒？

問：你問過你的家人沒有？ 答：還沒有，我今天晚上問。

1. 吃過／養生火鍋
2. 介紹過／節目
3. 做過／練習

(2) 不是…的問題，是…（上）的問題

問：是不是車子的問題？
答：不是車子大小的問題，是禮貌上的問題。

1. 錢／時間
2. 人／地方
3. 書／感覺

(3) 禮貌上先…一下

問：我應該先做什麼呢？
答：禮貌上先問一下。

1. 說
2. 拜訪
3. 打…招呼

(4) …，一定…死…了

例：你們那麼懂事，你們的接待家人一定愛死你們了！

1. 走了那麼多路／累
2. 早餐、中餐都沒吃／餓
3. 十個小孩子在一起／吵

【五‧漢字】

1.

2.

3.

字⇨ 詞⇨ 句⇨ 文

1 禮	送禮	想要**送**對**禮**物也是一種藝術。
	無禮	你已經不是小孩子了,怎麼還是那麼**無禮**?
	禮物	送**禮物**最重要的是心意。
	禮服	你穿這件**禮服**真漂亮!

下個月我的中文老師結婚,她邀請我去參加婚禮,我不要做一個**無禮**的外國人,所以想早一點準備好,應該怎麼**送禮**?送**禮物**還是禮金?要不要穿正式的**禮服**呢?

2 接	直接	我想你自己**直接**問他比較好。
	間接	這是別人**間接**交給我的。
	接送	每天按時**接送**孩子上下學。
	接近	那隻母狗太兇了,我們沒辦法**接近**那些小狗。

你每天都**接送**大老闆上下班,你是最**接近**他的人,可以**直接**問他這個問題,那不是很簡單嗎?為什麼還要**間接**請秘書問他?

3 價	物價	現在的**物價**,一天比一天高了。
	房價	這兩個地區的**房價**,差別好大!
	價值	愛情是沒辦法用**價值**去算的。
	價錢	你覺得這個**價錢**合理嗎?

這個**價錢**是二十年前的**房價**,二十年來**物價**漲了好幾倍,現在的**價值**一定不只三百萬了,如果你真的要買房子,就要快買,晚了就沒有這個**價錢**了!。

【六 · 練習】

(1) 重組 Jigsaw Sentences

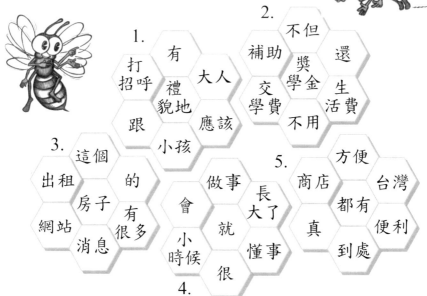

1. 打招呼 有禮貌地 大人 跟 應該 小孩

2. 補助 不但 獎學金 還 交學費 不用 生活費

3. 這個 出租 的 房子 有很多 網站 消息

4. 做事 會 長大了 就 小時候 很 懂事

5. 方便 商店 台灣 真 都有 便利 到處

(2) 說說看 Let's Talk

1. 他是誰？叫什麼名字？
2. 他是從哪裡來的？什麼時候來的？
3. 他是做什麼工作的？做多久了？
4. 他怎麼那麼會跳舞？怎麼學的？
5. 他為什麼那麼開心？中獎了嗎？

(3) 數來寶 — 我不要失禮：

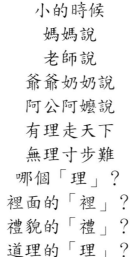

小的時候
媽媽說
老師說
爺爺奶奶說
阿公阿嬤說
有理走天下
無理寸步難
哪個「理」？
裡面的「裡」？
禮貌的「禮」？
道理的「理」？
還是那個木子「李」？
傻孩子
傻孫子
傻學生
做事要有「理」
做人要有「禮」
一定不失禮
在家輕鬆　隨便穿
出了大門　不隨便
師長在座　有坐相
長輩進門　要起讓
千萬要記得
有禮人人愛
無禮沒人愛
失禮更是大阻礙

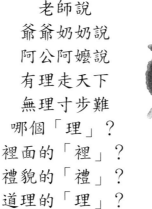

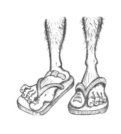

（1）在学校

得中：嗨！德美、欧福，这个周末我的接待家庭要带我去垦丁，你们要不要一起去？

德美：那么多人，方便吗？

欧福：你问过你的接待家人没有？

得中：还没有，可是他家有一部九人座的休旅车，可以坐九个人。

欧福：不是车子大小的问题，是礼貌上的问题。

德美：你最好先问问你的家人，如果可以，我们当然求之不得！

得中：对不起！我真不懂事，我应该先问他们，再问你们的。

（2）好消息！

德美：老师，刚才得中告诉我们一个好消息！

老师：什么好消息？

得中：我的接待家庭要带我们三个去垦丁玩！

老师：那太好了！你们一定会玩得很开心！

欧福：现在的油价那么高，我们应该付油钱，对不对？

老师：礼貌上先问一下，可是我想他们不会收。

德美：那我们应该做什么？

得中：我知道，我们可以买一点吃的、喝的，或是水果。

欧福：或是做几个德国口味的三明治。

老师：你们真懂事，你们的接待家人一定爱死你们了！

【八·拼音對照】

DÌ LIÙ KÈ　　JIĒDÀI JIĀ TÍNG

（1）Zài Xuéxiào

Dézhōng: Hāi! Déměi, Ōufú, zhège zhōumò wǒ de jiēdài jiātíng yào dài wǒ qù Kěndīng, nǐmen yào búyào yìqǐ qù?

Déměi: Nàme duō rén, fāngbiàn ma?

Ōufú: Nǐ wèn guò nǐ de jiēdài jiārén méiyǒu?

Dézhōng: Háiméiyǒu, kěshì tā jiā yǒu yíbù jiǔ rén zuò de xiūlǚ chē, kěyǐ zuò jiǔge rén.

Ōufú: Búshì chēzi dàxiǎo de wèntí, shì lǐmào shàng de wèntí.

Déměi: Nǐ zuìhǎo xiān wènwèn nǐ de jiārén, rúguǒ kěyǐ, wǒmen dāngrán qiú zhī bù de!

Dézhōng: Duìbùqǐ! Wǒ zhēn bù dǒngshì, wǒ yīnggāi xiān wèn tāmen, zài wèn nǐmen de.

(2) Hǎoxiāoxi!

Déměi: Lǎoshī, gāngcái Dézhōng gàosù wǒmen yíge hǎo xiāoxí!

Lǎoshī: Shéme hǎo xiāoxí?

Dézhōng: Wǒ de jiēdài jiātíng yào dài wǒmen sānge qù Kěndīng wán!

Lǎoshī: Nà tài hǎo le! Nǐmen yídìng huì wán de hěn kāixīn!

Ōufú: Xiànzài de yóujià nàme gāo, wǒmen yīnggāi fù yóuqián, duì búduì?

Lǎoshī: Lǐmào shàng xiān wèn yíxià, kěshì wǒ xiǎng tāmen búhuì shōu.

Déměi: Nà wǒmen yīnggāi zuò shémo?

Dézhōng: Wǒ zhīdào, wǒmen kěyǐ mǎi yìdiǎn chī de, hē de, huòshì shuǐguǒ.

Ōufú: Huòshì zuò jǐge Déguó kǒuwèi de sānmíngzhì.

Lǎoshī: Nǐmen zhēn dǒngshì, nǐmen de jiēdài jiārén yídìng àisǐ nǐmen le!

【九 · 英文翻譯】

◆ **Dialogue** – p. 73~74

(1) At School

Dezhong: Hi! Demei, Oufu, my host family is taking me to Kenting this weekend. Do you want to come along?

Demei: So many people! Would that be all right?

Oufu: Have you asked your host family yet?

Dezhong: Not yet, but they have a van that seats nine people.

Oufu: It's not a question of how big the car is, it's a question of what's polite.

Demei: It would be best if you first asked your family. If they say it's "okay", we'd be delighted to go along.

Dezhong: Sorry! I was so clueless. I should first ask them, and then invite you.

(2) Good News!

Demei: Teacher, just now Dezhong told us some good news!

Teacher: What good news is that?

Dezhong: My host family is going to take the three of us to Kenting!

Teacher: That's wonderful! You will certainly have a great time!

Oufu: With gas prices so high now, we should pay for the gas, shouldn't we?

Teacher: It's polite to ask, but I don't think they will accept your offer.

Demei: What should we do, then?

Dezhong: I know, we can buy some snacks, drinks, or fruit.

Oufu: Or we could make some German-style sandwiches.

Teacher: You are really catching on fast. Your host families are going to love you!

◆ Vocabulary – p. 75~76

1.	family	My family is very simple and small – only four people.
2.	receive, greet, treat	The host always treats guests hospitably.
3.	bring, take, carry	Where do you want to take the kids to play?
4.	Kenting National Park	Kenting is in southern Taiwan.
5.	van	Driving a van to travel in is very convenient.
6.	polite, courtesy	Be polite, then everyone will like you.

7.	weekend	I'm free this weekend. Do you want to go somewhere?
8.	seat	This seat is not very comfortable. Let's change.
9.	to understand worldly affairs	Kids don't know much, so don't be angry with them!
10.	to love (someone or something) "to death"	I love that little puppy! She really is very cute!
11.	flavor, taste	I would like to try every different flavor of cake.
12.	happy	I am very happy you think this way.
13.	gas price(s)	Recently, the price of oil has been getting higher every day.
14.	news, information	Why didn't you mention this news earlier?
15.	sandwich	What's in this sandwich? It's delicious!
16.	gas money	I don't even have enough money for food, so of course I don't have enough for gas!
17.	to be exactly what one wanted	This is what we asked for, so how could we say "no"?

◆ Grammar – p. 77

(1) Q: Have you asked your family yet?
　A: Not yet. I'll ask them this evening.
　1. Eaten yet / healthy, organic hot pot
　2. Introduced / program
　3. Did / exercise

(2) Q: Is there a problem with the car?
　A: It's not a question of the size of the car, it's a question of politeness.
　1. Money / time
　2. People / place
　3. Book(s) / feelings

(3) Q: What should I do first?　**A:** To be courteous, ask before acting.

1. Speak
2. Visit, courtesy call
3. Greet, address

(4) Example: You really know how things work! Your host families are going to love you!

1. Walking so far for so long / exhausted
2. Didn't eat breakfast or lunch / starving
3. Ten kids together / really noisy

◆ **Word to Sentence** – p. 78

1 禮	to send a gift	Thinking of the right gift to give is also a kind of art.
	impolite, rude	You are not a child any more, so how can you be so rude?
	gift, present	When giving a gift, it's the thought that counts most.
	formal attire	That gown you are wearing is beautiful!

My Chinese teacher is getting married next month, and has invited me to attend her wedding.　I don't want to look like an "impolite foreigner", so I am thinking ahead: "Should I send a gift?　Should I give a gift or money? Do I want to wear formal attire?"

2 接	direct(ly)	I think asking him directly yourself is better.
	indirect(ly)	Somebody gave me this through a third person.
	pick up and send	Every day I send my kids to school and pick them up afterwards.
	get close to, approach	That mother dog is too fierce, so there's no way to get close to her puppies.

Every day you chauffeur the boss to work, so you are the person closest to him.　You can ask him directly about this matter – wouldn't that be simple? Why bother going through his secretary to ask him?

3 價	the price of goods	The prices of things go up every day!
	housing prices	There are huge differences in housing prices between these two districts.

value, worth	It is impossible to calculate the value of love.
price	Do you feel this price is reasonable?

This price is what houses cost twenty years ago, and in these twenty years, commodity prices have increased by many times. The value today is certainly not just three million dollars, so if you really want to buy a house, you'd better buy it quickly, because later you won't get it for this price!

◆ **Practice** p. 80   Chant – **I Want to be Polite**

Listen to the teacher, and repeat each line three times. After becoming familiar with the rhythm, move on to the next section of the chant.

When I was small,

Momma said,

Teacher said

Grandfather, Grandmother said,

Grandpa, Grandma said,

"When you are polite, every corner of the world is your home;

"When you are rude, it's hard to move forward even an inch!"

Which "li" are we talking about?

Is it "inside" "li"?

"Courtesy" "li"?

"Reason" "li"?

Or the family name "Li"?

Oh my silly child,

My silly grandchild,

My silly student!

When dealing with affairs, you need to be reasonable.

When dealing with people you need to be courteous.

You won't go wrong with that attitude!

You can wear whatever you want to at home;

Be neat and clean when you step out of the house.

When teachers and older people are present,

Sit up straight!

When teachers and older people enter the room, you need to offer them your seat.

Remember!   For sure,

Everybody will love you when you are courteous;

No one will love when you're not!

Rudeness is a big obstacle in your social life.

第七課　台灣的交通

【一‧對話】

(1) 在路上

德美：　台灣的交通方便嗎？

老師：　大都市都很方便，鄉下就不一定了。

歐福：　我看每家都有摩托車。

得中：　好像還不只一部。

老師：　你們的觀察很正確，摩托車在台灣確實很方便。

德美：　啊！那部摩托車上坐了四個人！

老師：　那是很常見的，爸媽上下班的時候，順便接送孩子。

歐福：　這裡開車的人口應該也不少吧？

老師：　很多！只是市區開車要找停車位不容易。

　　　　如果要辦事情，多數人還是覺得騎車方便。

（2）過馬路

老師： 得中！小心！過馬路一定要停、看、聽。

得中： 哇，好險！謝謝老師救了我一命！

老師： 我也嚇了一跳，真是可怕。

歐福： 那個人沒戴安全帽又騎得那麼快，好危險！

老師： 每件事情都是有好有壞，騎摩托車方便但是危險。

德美： 老師，我們等的 77 路公車來了！

老師： 好，大家拿好零錢，準備上車了。

得中： 公車怎麼空空的，沒什麼人坐？

老師： 因為已經過了上班、上學的時段，

　　　還有很多人也覺得，

　　　等公車浪費時間，

　　　不方便，不願意坐。

	生詞	簡體字	詞類	拼音	英譯
1.	交通	交通	Adj.	jiāotōng	transportation, traffic
2.	都市	都市	N.	dūshì	city
3.	摩托車	摩托车	N.	mótuōchē	motorcycle
4.	不只	不只	Adv.	bùzhǐ	not only
5.	觀察	观察	N./V.	guānchá	observe, observation
6.	正確	正确	Adj.	zhèngquè	correct
7.	確實	确实	Adj.	quèshí	accurately, absolutely
8.	順便	顺便	Adj.	shùnbiàn	easily, handily
9.	接送	接送	V.	jiēsòng	pick up and drop off
10.	市區	市区	N.	shìqū	downtown area
11.	停車位	停车位	N.	tíngchēwèi	parking space
12.	辦事情	办事情	V.	bàn shìqíng	take care of business
13.	好險	好险	Adj.	hǎoxiǎn	very dangerous, close call
14.	救命	救命	V.	jiùmìng	HELP!, to save one's life
15.	嚇一跳	吓一跳	V.	xiàyítiào	to give one a fright
16.	可怕	可怕	Adj.	kěpà	frightening, fearsome
17.	戴安全帽	戴安全帽	V.	dài ānquán mào	to wear a safety helmet
18.	危險	危险	Adj.	wéixiǎn	danger, dangerous
19.	時段	时段	N.	shíduàn	a period of time
20.	浪費	浪费	V.	làngfèi	to waste

【三‧生詞用法】

請填入適當的生詞

1. 到外國，不只觀光還要_____那裡的人民生活。

2. _____ 生活比較有意思，也比較熱鬧。

3. 學生要_____懂了，老師才能教新課。

4. 我喜歡住在_____方便的地區。

5. 騎_____方便又便宜。

6. 你回來的時候，_____帶兩個便當回來。

7. 你們的觀察，不只_____還非常細心。

8. 我每天早上_____孩子上學，下午_____孩子放學。

9. 台灣_____好玩，還可以學好多正體字的故事。

10. 你為什麼站在黑黑的地方？_____了我_____。

11. 那個私人的停車場，有 100 個_____。

12. _____ ！沒被老師看見。

13. 你_____，我很放心。

14. _____ 啊！我不會游泳！

15. 騎摩托車一定要_____。

16. 上下班的_____，人多車也多。

17. 這是_____區，不能下水游泳。

18. 不要_____時間了，快點做功課。

19. 住在_____的好處是方便，壞處是太吵。

20. 剛才的事情好_____，我們以後要小心一點。

【四·語法】

(1) …是不是…？ 好像還不只…

問：我們以前是不是見過？ 答：對，好像還不只一次。
1. 有人在門口／兩個人
2. 來過這裡／一次
3. 喝了酒／一點

(2) …，…確實…

例：A：我覺得中文很難學。
　　B：你說對了，中文確實很難學。
1. 想法很正確／安全／重要
2. 說對了／事情／很麻煩
3. 我同意／台灣／好玩

(3) …沒…又…，好…！

問：為什麼危險？
答：他沒戴安全帽又騎得那麼快，好危險！
1. 親人／沒朋友／可憐
2. 沒水／沒電／麻煩
3. 功課／是週末／高興

(4) …好…，準備…了

例：整理好行李，準備出門了。
1. 洗手／吃飯
2. 做功課／睡覺
3. 穿衣服／上班

【五‧漢字】

1.

2.

3.

字⇨ 詞⇨ 句⇨ 文

1 時	準時	你說一個時間，我一定**準時**到。
	定時	吃飯**定時**定量，身體一定健康。
	時間	「沒有**時間**！」真是現代人的一個大問題。
	時段	上下班的**時段**，人車都很多。

你別跟人約在上下班的**時段**，雖然公車按**時間**，**定時**發車，可是碰到人多、車多的時候，你就不一定能**準時**到了。

2 順	孝順	孩子應該要**孝順**父母。
	通順	你寫的作文很**通順**。
	順利	祝你在國外一切都平安**順利**！
	順便	我可以**順便**買飲料回來。

寫作文跟說話一樣，最重要的就是**通順**。你這裡寫的「**順便孝順**父母」就不通了，對中國人來說，**孝順**父母是一件最重要的大事，不能**順便**做。你可以**順便**提醒你妹妹別忘了父母的生日，或是祝她學業**順利**。

3 怕	恐怕	這件事**恐怕**沒那麼簡單。
	可怕	鬼電影好**可怕**，我怕看那種影片。
	怕高	我從來不坐飛機，**我怕高**。
	怕熱	他天不怕地不怕，就**怕熱**。

我們都知道熱不**可怕**，高也不**可怕**，可是胖子**怕熱**，高個子**怕高**。**恐怕**這是沒辦法改變的事實。

【六·練習】

（1）你問我答

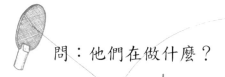

例：　　問：他們在做什麼？

答：他們在等公車。

問：

　1. 他們在哪裡等公車？
　2. 有多少人在那裡？
　3. 那位先生在想什麼？
　4. 他為什麼不高興？
　5. 你想他們急不急？
　6. 公車為什麼還沒來？
　7. 從你家坐公車到學校，要多久時間？
　8. 台灣計程車起跳多少錢？每跳一次多少錢？
　9. 如果你等公車等了很久，時間快來不及了，你怎麼辦？

(2) 看圖說故事

蔡光輝 攝

1. 市區中常常看到這樣的告示牌。
2. 工作人員一定要戴安全帽，確實很麻煩，可是比較安全。
3. 這個公車站有很多公車可以坐，好像還不止三班。
4. 在台灣很多父母下班時，才順便接孩子回家。
5. 這裡空氣真好，沒車又沒什麼人，好安靜！

（1）在路上

德美： 台湾的交通方便吗？

老师： 大都市都很方便，乡下就不一定了。

欧福： 我看每家都有摩托车。

得中： 好像还不只一部。

老师： 你们的观察很正确，摩托车在台湾确实很方便。

德美： 啊！那部摩托车上坐了四个人！

老师： 那是很常见的，爸妈上下班的时候，顺便接送孩子。

欧福： 这里开车的人口应该也不少吧？

老师： 很多！只是市区开车要找停车位不容易。如果要办事情，多数人还是觉得骑车方便。

（2）过马路

老师： 得中！小心！过马路一定要停、看、听。

得中： 哇，好险！谢谢老师救了我一命！

老师： 我也吓了一跳，真是可怕。

欧福： 那个人没戴安全帽又骑得那么快，好危险！

老师： 每件事情都是有好有坏，骑摩托车方便但是危险。

德美： 老师，我们等的77路公交车来了！

老师： 好，大家拿好零钱，准备上车了。

得中： 公交车怎么空空的，没什么人坐？

老师： 因为已经过了上班、上学的时段，还有很多人也觉得，等公交车浪费时间，不方便，不愿意坐。

【八·拼音對照】

DÌ QĪ KÈ　　TÁIWĀN DE JIĀOTŌNG

（1）Zài Lù Shàng

Déměi：　 Táiwān de jiāotōng fāngbiàn ma?

Lǎoshī：　 Dàdūshì hěn fāngbiàn, xiāngxià jiù bùyídìng le .

Ōufú：　 Wǒ kàn měi jiā dōu yǒu mótuōchē.

Dézhōng： Hǎoxiàng hái bùzhǐ yíbù.

Lǎoshī:	Nǐmen de guānchá hěn zhèngquè, mótuōchē zài Táiwān quèshí hěn fāngbiàn.
Déměi:	A! Nèibù mótuōchē shàngmiàn zuò le sìge rén!
Lǎoshī:	Nàshì hěn chángjiàn de, bàmā shàngxiàbān de shíhòu, shùnbiàn jiēsòng háizi.
Ōufú:	Zhèlǐ kāichē de rénkǒu yīnggāi yě bùshǎo ba?
Lǎoshī:	Hěnduō! Zhǐshì shìqū kāichē yào zhǎo tíngchēwèi bù róngyì. Rúguǒ yào bàn shìqíng, duōshù rén háishì juéde qíchē fāngbiàn.

(2) Guò Mǎlù

Lǎoshī:	Dézhōng! Xiǎoxīn! Guò mǎlù yídìng yào tíng, kàn, tīng.
Dézhōng:	Wa, hǎoxiǎn! Xièxie Lǎoshī jiù le wǒ yí mìng!
Lǎoshī:	Wǒ yě xià le yí tiào, zhēnshì kěpà.
Ōufú:	Nàge rén méi dài ānquánmào yòu qí de nàme kuài, hǎo wéixiǎn!
Lǎoshī:	Měijiàn shìqíng dōushì yǒu hǎo yǒu huài, qí mótuōchē fāngbiàn dànshì wéixiǎn.
Déměi:	Lǎoshī, wǒmen děng de 77 lù gōngchē lái le!
Lǎoshī:	Hǎo, dàjiā ná hǎo língqián, zhǔnbèi shàng chē le.
Dézhōng:	Gōngchē zěnme kōngkōng de, méi shéme rén zuò?
Lǎoshī:	Yīnwèi yǐjīng guò le shàngbān, shàngxué de shíduàn, háiyǒu hěn duō rén yě juéde, děng gōngchē làngfèi shíjiān, bù fāngbiàn, bú yuànyì zuò.

【九 · 英文翻譯】

◆ **Dialogue** – p. 87~88

(1) Along the Road

Demei:	Is transportation convenient in Taiwan?
Teacher:	It's convenient in the big cities, but in the countryside, it depends.
Oufu:	I see that every family has a motorcycle.

Dezhong: It looks like they each have more than one.

Teacher: Your observations are pretty accurate! Motorcycles certainly are convenient in Taiwan.

Demei: Ah! There are four people on that motorcycle!

Teacher: That's a pretty common sight. When parents go to or from work, they send or pick up their children while en route.

Oufu: The number of people driving cars here is also pretty big, isn't it?

Teacher: There are a LOT! It's just that it's not easy to find a parking space downtown. If you need to run some errands, most people still feel riding a motorcycle is more convenient.

(2) Crossing the Road

Teacher: Be careful, Dezhong! When crossing the road you must stop, look, and listen!

Dezhong: Wow, that was a close call! Thank you, Teacher, for "saving my life"!

Teacher: I was startled, too. How frightening!

Oufu: That person is speeding on a motorcycle without wearing a helmet. That's really dangerous!

Teacher: Everything has its good and bad sides. Motorcycles are convenient, but they're also dangerous.

Demei: Teacher, bus 77, the one we've been waiting for, is coming.

Teacher: Okay, everybody get your change ready, and prepare to get on the bus.

Dezhong: Why is the bus so empty? Not many people riding!

Teacher: That's because it's already past time for everybody to go to work and school. Also, a lot of people feel that riding buses is a waste of time and inconvenient, so they'd rather not ride them.

◆ **Vocabulary – p. 91**

1. observe, observation — When going abroad, don't just sightsee, but also observe how the people live.
2. city — City life is more interesting and full of activity.

3.	accurately, absolutely	Students absolutely need to understand (the lesson) before the teacher can move on to a new one.
4.	transportation, traffic	I like to live in an area where the transportation is convenient.
5.	motorcycle	Riding motorcycles is both convenient and inexpensive.
6.	easily, handily	When you return, pick up a couple of lunch boxes en route.
7.	correct	Your observations are not only correct, but also precise.
8.	pick up and drop off	Every morning, I send the kids to school, and in the afternoon I pick them up.
9.	not only	Taiwan is not only fun, but you can also learn so many stories about traditional Chinese characters.
10.	to give one a fright	Why were you standing there in the dark? You scared me!
11.	parking space	That privately-owned parking lot has one hundred parking spaces.
12.	very dangerous, close call	What a close call! Fortunately, the teacher didn't see it.
13.	take care of business	When you are taking care of business, I have no worries.
14.	HELP!, to save one's life	Help! I can't swim!
15.	to wear a safety helmet	When riding a motorcycle, you certainly must wear a motorcycle helmet.
16.	a period of time	During the times for going to or leaving work, there are lots of people and cars.
17.	danger, dangerous	This is a dangerous area, so you cannot go into the water to swim.
18.	to waste	Don't waste time, hurry up and do your homework.
19.	downtown area	The good thing about living downtown is the convenience; the bad thing is the noise.
20.	frightening, fearsome	The thing that just happened was frightening! We need to be more careful in the future.

◆ Grammar – p. 92

(1) Q: Have we met before?
 A: Yes, and it seems like more than one time.
 1. Are there people at the door / two people
 2. Been here before / once
 3. Drank wine / a little

(2) Q: I feel that Chinese is hard to study / learn.
 A: You've said it! Chinese really isn't easy to learn / study.
 1. Way of thinking is correct / safety / important
 2. You've said it / business / trouble
 3. I agree / Taiwan / a lot of fun

(3) Q: Why did you say that riding motorcycles is dangerous?
 A: Look at that person who isn't wearing a safety helmet and is speeding, too. That's so dangerous!
 1. Relative / doesn't have any friends / to be pitied
 2. Water / electricity/ troublesome
 3. Homework / it's the weekend / happy

(4) Example: After the suitcases are packed, we can get ready to go.
 1. Hands washed / eat
 2. Homework finished / sleep
 3. Get dressed / go to work

◆ Word to Sentence – p. 93

1 時	on schedule, prompt(ly)	You tell me the time, and I will certainly be there.
	fixed time(s)	Eating set amounts of food at fixed times is certainly good for one's health.
	time	"Lack of time" is modern people's greatest problem.

	period of time	During the rush hours, there are too many crowds and too much traffic.

Don't make an appointment to meet someone during peak traffic periods, because even though buses may be running on schedule, there will be too many people and too much traffic, so you can't be certain to arrive on time.

2 順	filial	Children should be filial to their parents.
	smooth(ly), fluently	You write very well.
	smooth(ly)	I hope everything goes smoothly for you while you're abroad!
	convenient, at one's convenience	I can buy drinks on my way back without any trouble or inconvenience.

Writing a composition is just like speaking: the most important thing is smoothness and fluency. What you've written here, "Being Filial to One's Parents when it's Convenient" is really unacceptable. According to the Chinese point of view, being filial to one's parents is the most important thing, not something you can do "whenever it's convenient"! You can, at your own convenience, remind your sister not to forget your parent's birthdays, or to wish her smooth progress in her studies.

3 怕	to fear, be afraid	I'm afraid this matter isn't that simple.
	fearsome, terrible	Ghost movies are really scary, and I'm afraid to watch that kind of film.
	to be afraid of heights	I have never flown in an airplane, because I'm afraid of heights.
	to be intolerant of heat	He fears nothing, but he is afraid of heat.

We all know that heat and heights aren't in themselves terrible, but some people are afraid of heat and others fear high places. I'm afraid that's just a fact that we can't change.

第八課　吃飯皇帝大

【一‧對話】

(1) 在吃飯

德美：　請你把這本書拿給小王。

得中：　老師說：「吃飯皇帝大」。吃飯的時候是不可以打擾
　　　　的。我等一下再拿給他。

歐福：　老師，吃飯跟皇帝有什麼關係？

老師：　我們覺得吃飯是最重要的事情，就好像皇帝一樣，你
　　　　當然不能在皇帝吃飯的時候打擾他。

德美：　懂了。那麼請你吃完飯，把這本書拿給小王，好嗎？

得中：　好。沒問題。

德美：　我也要吃飯了，吃飯皇帝大，請不要打擾我。

(2) 客氣話

德美： 老師，我們只有三個人來吃飯，你為什麼準備這麼多菜呢？

老師： 沒什麼菜，沒什麼菜，大家多吃一點兒。

得中： 那麼多菜，為什麼說沒什麼菜呢？

老師： 這是客氣話。送禮物給朋友的時候，我們也常說這不是什麼貴重的東西，小意思、小東西請收下。

歐福： 這跟我們很不一樣。

老師： 我做這麼多菜，是因為歡迎你們。再加上我們喜歡熱鬧，人越多越好。

得中： 難怪台灣人吃飯的時候，聊天的聲音特別大。

	生詞	簡體字	詞類	拼音	英譯
1.	皇帝	皇帝	N.	huángdì	emperor
2.	關係	关系	N.	guānxi	relationship
3.	重要	重要	Adj.	zhòngyào	important
4.	好像	好像	Adv.	hǎoxiàng	look like
5.	做事	做事	V.	zuòshì	do things, take care of business
6.	準備	准备	V.	zhǔnbèi	prepare, get ready
7.	客氣話	客气话	N.	kèqìhuà	polite expression
8.	送	送	V.	sòng	send, give
9.	禮物	礼物	N.	lǐwù	gift, present
10.	收下	收下	V.	shōuxià	receive, accept
11.	歡迎	欢迎	V.	huānyíng	welcome
12.	加上	加上	Adv.	jiāshàng	to add on
13.	熱鬧	热闹	Adj.	rènào	hubbub
14.	難怪	难怪	Adv.	nánguài	no wonder
15.	聲音	声音	N.	shēngyīn	voice, sound, noise
16.	特別	特别	Adj.	tèbié	special

請填入適當的生詞

1. 我早上打掃房間、洗衣服，已經____了很多____了。
2. 我和他是朋友_____。
3. 學中文最_____的是「說」。
4. 我說的話，我的狗_____都聽懂了。
5. 明天旅行的行李，都_____好了嗎？
6. 你知道中國最後的一個_____是誰嗎？
7. 在台灣不要_____傘給女朋友，因為可能分手。
8. 他很喜歡說_____，有的時候不知道什麼是真的。
9. 他什麼都有，送他什麼生日_____比較好呢？
10. 這是我從日本買回來的小禮物，請你_____。
11. _____你有空來我家玩。
12. 他走路的_____好大聲啊。
13. 台灣的夜市每天都非常_____。
14. 今天是我的生日，所以媽媽_____做了蛋糕。
15. 你今天穿得很漂亮，再_____一頂帽子就更漂亮了。
16. A：他昨天錢包丟了。B：_____昨天他不跟我去吃飯。

【四‧語法】

(1) …跟…有/沒(有)關係

問：這件事跟他有沒有關係？　答：這件事跟他沒關係。

1. 他沒來上課／考試
2. 他喜歡音樂／他小時候學鋼琴
3. 你來台灣學中文／你的朋友

(2) …好像…一樣

問：她寫的漢字怎麼樣？
答：她寫的漢字好像老師寫的一樣。

1. 我媽媽做的菜／餐廳做的
2. 妳的新房子／皇宮
3. 那裡的氣氛／過年

(3) …(沒)有什麼

問：今天家裡有什麼好吃的菜嗎？
答：今天家裡沒有什麼好吃的菜。

1. 這附近／好玩的地方
2. 我已經有很多書了／要買的書
3. 該做的我都做完了／要做的事

(4) …因為…，再加上…

問：你今天為什麼沒來考試？
答：因為我生病了，再加上這幾天忙，沒看書。

1. 你昨晚沒睡好嗎？　　我喝了咖啡／隔壁的小孩吵
2. 他怎麼不騎摩托車？　騎摩托車危險／他也沒錢買車
3. 你還沒準備好嗎？　　時間來不及／事情太多

【五‧漢字】

1.

2.

3.

字⇨ 詞⇨ 句⇨ 文

1 氣	生氣	別**生氣**了，**生氣**對身體不好。
	客氣	他對人總是很**客氣**。
	氣氛	這裡的**氣氛**很好，可以多坐一下。
	氣球	為什麼每個小朋友都喜歡**氣球**？

　　有**氣球**的地方，**氣氛**總是很好，特別是有氣球又有小孩子的時候，更是充滿了**生氣**，每個人都很**客氣**，都沒有人**生氣**。

2 音	聲音	這個**聲音**太大了，小聲一點好嗎？
	錄音	我們去海邊**錄音**，錄海的聲音。
	音樂	一邊聽**音樂**，一邊看書，多麼享受！
	音響	我換了一套新的**音響**，晚上來我家聽音樂吧！

　　製作**音樂**的**錄音**室，裡面的**音響**是最高品質的，每一種高低的**聲音**，**錄音**師都可以聽得很清楚。

3 當	便當	中午吃**便當**，方便又便宜。
	上當	你別**上當**了，他是騙你的。
	當然	吃了便當**當然**要付錢。
	當中	站在**當中**的那位就是校長。

　　我吃了十年的**便當**，在這十年**當中**，**當然上過當**、吃到過不新鮮的**便當**。

【六・練習】

（1）你問我答

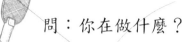

例： 問：你在做什麼？

答：（我）沒做什麼。

問：你有什麼問題？　　　答：（我）沒什麼問題。
問：你有什麼事？　　　　答：（我）沒什麼事。
問：你買了幾本書？　　　答：（我）沒買幾本（書）。
問：你吃了幾個水餃？　　答：（我）沒吃幾個（水餃）。
問：你有幾件衣服？　　　答：（我）沒幾件（衣服）。
問：你們班有幾個學生？　答：（我們班）沒幾個（學生）。
問：你有多少錢？　　　　答：（我）沒多少（錢）。
問：你跟誰去？　　　　　答：（我）沒跟誰去。
問：你昨天去哪裡了？　　答：（我）沒去哪裡。

（2）魔鏡

前　面　前
馬　上　馬
法　律　法
法　文　電
電　台　對
對　面

前　面　前
馬　上　馬
法　律　法
電　文　電
對　台　對
　　面

(3) 看圖說故事 – 停看聽

A 圖.

問：1.他是誰？叫什麼名字？
　　2.他是從哪裡來的？
　　　什麼時候來的？
　　3.他是做什麼工作的？
　　　做多久了？
　　4.他怎麼那麼急？要去哪裡？
　　5.他為什麼要坐計程車？

答：(我想是因為…，再加上…)

B 圖.

問：1.她是誰？叫什麼名字？
　　2.她是做什麼工作的？
　　　做多久了？
　　3.她喜歡這份工作嗎？為什麼？
　　4.她為什麼要加班？
　　　做不完怎麼辦？
　　5.她怎麼有那麼多工作？

答：(我想是因為…，再加上…)

C 圖.

問：1.她是誰？叫什麼名字？
　　2.她是做什麼工作的？
　　　做多久了？
　　3.她跟她男朋友認識多久了？
　　4.她為什麼哭？
　　5.她男朋友為什麼要跟她分手？

答：(我想是因為…，再加上…)

（1）在吃饭

德美： 请你把这本书拿给小王。

得中： 老师说：吃饭皇帝大。吃饭的时候是不可以打扰的。
我等一下再拿给他。

欧福： 老师，吃饭跟皇帝有什么关系？

老师： 我们觉得吃饭是最重要的事情，就好像皇帝一样，你
当然不能在皇帝吃饭的时候打扰他。

德美： 懂了。那么请你吃完饭，把这本书拿给小王，好吗？

得中： 好。没问题。

德美： 我也要吃饭了，吃饭皇帝大，请不要打扰我。

（2）客气话

德美： 老师，我们只有三个人来吃饭，你为什么准备这么多
菜呢？

老师： 没什么菜，没什么菜，大家多吃一点儿。

得中： 那么多菜，为什么说没什么菜呢？

老师： 这是客气话。送礼物给朋友的时候，我们也常说这不
是什么贵重的东西，小意思、小东西请收下。

欧福： 这跟我们很不一样。

老师： 我做这么多菜，是因为欢迎你们。再加上我们喜欢热
闹，人越多越好。

得中： 难怪台湾人吃饭的时候，聊天的声音特别大。

【八‧拼音對照】

DÌ BĀ KÈ　　CHĪFÀN HUÁNGDÌ DÀ

（1）Zài Chīfàn

Déměi：　　Qǐng nǐ bǎ zhèběn shū nágěi XiǎoWáng.

Dézhōng：Lǎoshī shuō：chīfàn huángdì dà. Chīfàn de shíhòu
shì bù kěyǐ dǎrǎo de. Wǒ děng yíxià zài nágěi tā.

Ōufú：　　Lǎoshī, chīfàn gēn huángdì yǒu shéme guānxi?

Lǎoshī: Wǒmen juéde chīfàn shì zuì zhòngyào de shìqíng,
             jiù hǎoxiàng huángdì yíyang, nǐ dāngrán bù léng zài
             huángdì chīfàn de shíhòu dǎrǎo tā.
Déměi: Dǒng le.   Nàme qǐngnǐ chīwán fàn, bǎ zhèběn shū
             nágěi XiǎoWáng, hǎoma?
Dézhōng: Hǎo.   Méi wèntí.
Déměi: Wǒ yěyào chīfàn le, chīfàn huángdì dà, qǐng búyào
             dǎrǎo wǒ.

(2) Kèqì Huà
  Déměi: Lǎoshī, wǒmēn zhǐyǒu sānge rén lái chīfàn, nǐ wèi
             shéme zhǔnbèi zhème duō cài ne?
  Lǎoshī: Méi shéme cài, méi shéme cài, dàjiā duō chī
             yìdiǎnr.
  Dézhōng: Nàme duō cài, wèi shéme shuō méi shéme cài ne?
  Lǎoshī: Zhèshì kèqì huà.   Sòng lǐwù gěi péngyǒu de
             shíhòu, wǒmen yě cháng shuō zhè búshì shéme
             guìzhòng de dōngxi, xiǎo yìsi, xiǎo dōngxi qǐng
             shōuxià.
  Ōufú: Zhè gēn wǒmen hěn bù yíyàng.
  Lǎoshī: Wǒ zuò zhème duō cài, shì yīnwèi huānyíng nǐmen.
             Zài jiāshàng wǒmen xǐhuān rènào, rén yuèduō
             yuèhǎo.
  Dézhōng: Nánguài Táiwān rén chīfàn de shíhòu, liáotiān de
             shēngyīn tèbié dà.

【九 · 英文翻譯】

◆ **Dialogue** – p. 101~102

(1) Eating
Demei: Please give this book to Xiao Wang.
Dezhong: Teacher has said, "When I'm eating, I am like an emperor, and
           cannot be disturbed." I will give it to him later.
Oufu: Teacher, what do "emperor" and "eating" have to do with each
           other?

Teacher: We feel that eating is the most important thing, just like the emperor is the most important person. Of course, you cannot disturb the emperor while he is eating!

Demei: I understand. After you've finished eating, would you then please give Xiao Wang this book?

Dezhong: Okay. No problem!

Demei: Now I'm going to eat. Like an emperor! Please do not disturb me!

(2) Polite Remarks

Demei: Teacher, we only have three people who have come to eat, why did you prepare so much food?

Teacher: It's nothing fancy. Please, help yourselves!

Dezhong: So many dishes! Why do you say it's "nothing fancy"?

Teacher: This is just a polite expression. When we give friends a gift, we usually say, "This is nothing valuable, a mere trifle."

Oufu: This is very different from our culture.

Teacher: I prepared all these dishes just to welcome you. Also, we like a lot of "hubbub" – the more people, the better.

Dezhong: No wonder, when people in Taiwan eat together, they're LOUD!

◆ **Vocabulary** – p. 103~104

1.	do things, take care of business	This morning I cleaned the house and did the laundry, so I've already done a lot.
2.	relationship	We have a friendly relationship.
3.	important	"Speaking" is the most important part of learning Chinese.
4.	look like	My dog looks like it understood what I said.
5.	prepare, get ready	Is the luggage ready for tomorrow's trip?
6.	emperor	Do you know who the last Chinese emperor was?
7.	send, give	In Taiwan, you can't give your girlfriend an umbrella, because it means you might break up.
8.	polite expression	He likes to speak politely, so it's hard to know when he's sincere.

9.	gift, present	He's got everything already! What can we give him as a birthday present?
10.	receive, accept	Please accept this little present I brought back from Japan.
11.	welcome	Whenever you have some free time, feel welcome to come to my house.
12.	voice, sound, noise	He makes a lot of noise when he walks.
13.	hubbub	Night markets in Taiwan are always active, crowded and noisy.
14.	special	Today's my birthday, so Mom made a special cake.
15.	to add on	Your outfit today is very pretty. If you added a hat, you'd look even better!
16.	no wonder	A: He lost his wallet yesterday. B: No wonder he didn't want to go out to eat with me!

◆ Grammar – p. 105

(1) To have something to do with….
Q: Does this matter have anything to do with him?
A: This business has nothing to do with him.
  1. He didn't come to class / take a test
  2. He likes music / he studied piano when he was young
  3. You came to Taiwan to study Chinese / your friend

(2) …looks a lot like…
Q: How does she write Chinese characters ?
A: She writes Chinese characters that look a lot like the teacher's.
  1. My mother cooks food / like a restaurant's
  2. Your new house / palace
  3. The atmosphere there / New Year

(3) … not (have) something…

Q: What do we have at home today that's good to eat?

A: We don't have anything at home today that's good to eat.

  1. Near here / fun, interesting place(s)

  2. I already have so many books / need to buy any books

  3. I've already done everything I wanted to do / need to do any more

(4) …is because…and furthermore…

Q: Why didn't you come to the test today?

A: I didn't take the test because I was sick, and furthermore, I've been too busy these last few days to study.

  1. Didn't you sleep yesterday?

    I drank coffee / next door neighbors' child was noisy

  2. Why doesn't he ride a motorcycle? riding a motorcycle is dangerous / he doesn't have enough money to buy one

  3. Aren't you ready yet? I don't have enough time / too much to do

◆ Word to Sentence – p. 106

1 氣	to get angry	Don't get angry, because anger harms your health.
	polite, politeness	He is always very polite to everyone.
	mood, ambience	The ambience here is very nice, so let's stay a little longer.
	balloon	Why do all children like balloons?

  Wherever there are balloons, the atmosphere is very nice, especially when there are balloons and children.　That place is full of energy; everybody is so polite and nobody gets angry.

2 音	sound, voice	This sound is too loud!　Could you lower the volume a little?
	record, recording	Let's go to the beach to record the sound of the ocean.
	music	Listening to music while reading is such a great pleasure!
	audio system	I've replaced my sound system, so this evening you can come to my house to listen to music!

In professional recording studios, the audio systems are of the highest quality.   The sound engineer can hear every high and every low perfectly clearly.

3 當	lunch box	Eating a box lunch at noontime is both convenient and inexpensive.
	to be taken in, be fooled	Don't be taken in! He is fooling / cheating you!
	of course, naturally	If you eat a box lunch, of course you have to pay for it.
	in the middle, during	The person standing in the middle is the school president.

I've been eating boxed lunches for ten years, and during this ten years, of course I've been taken in a few times, and eaten some boxed lunches that weren't very fresh.

蔡光輝 攝

1. 這是蔡先生拍的，難怪拍得這麼好！
2. 這裡的風景很美，難怪人人都想來這裡旅遊。

閱讀（二）

　　很多來台灣的觀光客都一定要去阿里山。阿里山為什麼那麼有名？我想因為阿里山有很老的大樹，我們叫它「神木」；天還沒亮大家就等著看太陽出來，我們說「看日出」；還有「雲海」和世界三大「登山鐵路」之一的森林火車。

　　如果你想去阿里山，可以搭車到嘉義，然後換客運車到阿里山，或是搭森林火車上山。從嘉義到阿里山大約兩個半小時左右，在車站常有不認識的人要你搭他的車，你不搭他的車，他就一直跟著你，像這樣的黃牛車也很多，要特別小心。

　　週末或放假的時候去阿里山的人特別多，如果你想在山上住一個晚上，最好先打電話訂房間。有些人喜歡在新年的時候去阿里山看日出，有些人喜歡在春天三、四月的時候去阿里山看櫻花。

　　任何一個季節去阿里山都有它不同的美景。春天賞花，夏天健行，秋天看雲海，冬天看日出，你喜歡哪個季節去？打算什麼時候邀幾個好朋友去阿里山走一走呢？

1. 為什麼很多觀光客來台灣一定要去阿里山呢？
2. 為什麼在車站常有黃牛車呢？
3. 去阿里山要注意些什麼？雲海是什麼？賞花又是什麼？

複習（二）

一、選擇

1. 我明天有事，你_____（①方便 ②當然 ③習慣）後天來嗎？

2. 你說的對，台灣的交通_____（①正確 ②確實 ③觀察）很亂。

3. A：他剛剛已經吃了三個包子了。

   B：_____（①建議 ②聽說 ③難怪）叫他吃飯，他說他不餓。

4. 我下午要去市區_____（①辦 ②做 ③送）事情。

5. 阿英的女兒一回家就幫忙整理家裡，真是一個_____（①特別
   ②懂事 ③禮貌）的孩子。

6. 這是法國的香水，你聞聞看，喜歡不喜歡這種_____（①味道
   ②口味 ③氣氛）？

二、重組

1. ①很漂亮 ②台灣 ③風景 ④聽說 ⑥的 ⑦南部 ⑧我。

   _____

2. ①昨天晚上 ②再加上 ③沒睡好 ④所以 ⑤是因為
   ⑥考得不好 ⑦沒念書 ⑧沒考好。

   _____

3. ①餐廳 ②好吃 ③一樣 ④她 ⑤好像 ⑥做的菜 ⑦做的菜。

   _____

4. ①你要開車 ②求之不得 ③載我 ④真的是 ⑤來說 ⑥去學校
   ⑦對我。

   _____

5. ①台北 ②高雄 ③五個小時 ④大約 ⑤開車 ⑥從 ⑦要 ⑧
   到。

   _____

第九課　補　補　補！

【一・對話】

（1）去補習

小文：　對不起，我今天晚上要補習，不能跟你們出去玩了。

歐福：　你已經是大學生了，為什麼還要去補習？

德美：　因為她要考研究所。

得中：　考研究所不能自己準備嗎？

小文：　當然可以，只是我比較懶，去補習班，老師會幫我們
　　　　整理重點。

德美：　小文，你一點都不懶！

得中：　就是啊！白天上課，晚上還要去補習班。

歐福：　對我們來說，那是不可能的事情！

小文：　我們已經習慣了，從小補到大。我得走了，拜拜！

（2）補一補

得中： 昨天聽小文說「從小補到大」，我們不太懂意思，就上網查資料。

老師： 你們查到了什麼資料？

德美： 好多！像是補課、補考、補票、補洞、補交作業、補充水份，這些都好懂。

得中： 可是對補一補、吃補、補血、補氣、補身體，就不太清楚了。

老師： 基本上「補」有「完、好」的意思，如果有不夠、不全的情形，就需要補全它。

德美： 為什麼要「從小補到大」呢？

老師： 因為人從小時候到大，應該說「到老」，身體如果缺少了什麼？醫師會建議吃不同的維他命。我們中醫就會建議除了藥補之外，還要食補。

得中： 哦！所以精神不好，就要喝雞精補充精力，是嗎？

老師： 學得真快！看來今天下午可以不用補課了！

【二·生詞】

	生詞	簡體字	詞類	拼音	英譯
1.	補習	补习	V.	bǔxí	"cram", to do supplemental studies
2.	教育	教育	N.	jiàoyù	education
3.	研究所	研究所	N.	yánjiùsuǒ	graduate school
4.	懶	懒	Adj.	lǎn	lazy
5.	整理	整理	V.	zhěnglǐ	organize, arrange, tidy
6.	重點	重点	N.	zhòngdiǎn	an important point
7.	剛	刚	Adv.	gāng	just now
8.	上網	上网	V.	shàngwǎng	get on the Internet
9.	查	查	V.	chá	look up, check
10.	資料	资料	N.	zīliào	information
11.	補充	补充	V.	bǔchōng	to make up a deficiency, to replenish
12.	水份	水份	N.	shuǐfèn	water content, moisture
13.	基本	基本	Adj.	jīběn	essentially, basically
14.	不全	不全	Adj.	bùquán	incomplete
15.	缺少	缺少	Adj.	quēshǎo	lack
16.	醫師	医师	N.	yīshī	physician
17.	維他命	维他命	N.	wéitāmìng	vitamin
18.	精神	精神	N.	jīngshén	spirits, energy
19.	雞精	鸡精	N.	jījīng	essence of chicken broth

【三・生詞用法】

請填入適當的生詞

1. 我唸＿＿＿＿＿＿的時候，已經開始工作了。

2. 你太＿＿＿＿＿＿了吧！睡到中午十二點。

3. 我們應該天天＿＿＿＿＿＿房間。

4. 請你趕快說＿＿＿＿＿＿。

5. 我＿＿＿＿＿＿買了一張地圖。

6. 補習＿＿＿＿＿＿在亞洲很流行。

7. 不只學生，成人也去補習班＿＿＿＿＿＿。

8. 現在大學生＿＿＿＿＿＿的時間比說話的時間多。

9. 你給的基本資料＿＿＿＿＿＿，請明天補全。

10. 別的＿＿＿＿＿＿我明天再補交，可以嗎？

11. 爬山的時候，要隨時補充＿＿＿＿＿＿。

12. ＿＿＿＿＿＿ 上我們的想法是一樣的。

13. 還有沒有人要＿＿＿＿＿＿說明的？

14. 你是上哪一個網站＿＿＿＿＿＿的？

15. 精神不好，喝＿＿＿＿＿＿有用嗎？

16. 請告訴我還＿＿＿＿＿＿什麼資料？

17. 你今天的＿＿＿＿＿＿比昨天好多了。

18. 不喜歡戶外活動的人，常缺少＿＿＿＿＿＿D。

19. 你應該請教＿＿＿＿＿＿，不要自己隨便吃藥。

【四・語法】

(1)...一點都不/沒...

問：你想去嗎？　答：我一點都不想去。
　　1. 想試試嗎？
　　2. 有興趣嗎？
　　3. 知道嗎？

(2) 對...來說，那是不可能...

問：你覺得早上六點怎麼樣？
答：對多數人來說，那是不可能的時間。
　　1. 學生不交作業？　　老師／接受
　　2. 小孩不上學？　　　父母／答應
　　3. 打對折？　　　　　老闆／事情

(3) 除了...之外，還...。

問：你想加強學習什麼？
答：除了加強會話能力之外，還想學書法。
　　1. 為什麼來台灣？
　　2. 為什麼要吃補？
　　3. 出國的目的是什麼？

(4) 看來...了！

問：他為什麼還沒來？　答：看來他今天不會來了！
　　1. 風雨這麼大，是不是有颱風？
　　2. 他那麼開心，是不是通過考試了？
　　3. 老師為什麼不說話？

【五·漢字】

1.

2.

3.

字⇨　詞⇨　句⇨　文

1 補	填補	快把這個洞**填補**好。
	進補	從前老年人有冬天**進補**的習慣。
	補藥	這是給病人吃的**補藥**。
	補習	現在幾乎每個中學生，放了學都要去**補習**。

　　你應該要**吃**一點**補**的東西了，那麼瘦，最近又常常生病，可能是每天白天上課，晚上還要去補習班**補習**，把身體都累壞了。我聽說冬天**進補**最有效，剛才就去中藥店，買了一些**補藥**來給你補補身體。

2 教	家教	「**家教**」有家庭教育，也有家庭教師的意思。
	宗教	每一個人都有**宗教**的自由。
	教室	這間**教室**的空間跟光線都很好。
	教書	**教書**是一份很好的工作。

　　他父母都是**教書**的，所以**家教**很嚴，規定他放學以後，一定要在**教室**裡做完功課才能回家，每天都要看半個小時關於**宗教**方面的書。

3 好	問好	幫我跟你家人**問好**。
	嗜好	我的**嗜好**是爬山、聽音樂。
	好意	他是**好意**，你就不要生他的氣了
	好事	這是**好事**，我當然願意幫忙。

　　你回鄉下的時候，幫我**問**你爸爸媽媽**好**。我記得你爸爸沒什麼**嗜好**，就是喜歡喝酒，其實每天能喝一點小酒是**好事**，就是別喝過量，我是**好意**勸他，請他別生氣！

【六‧練習】

(1) 說說看

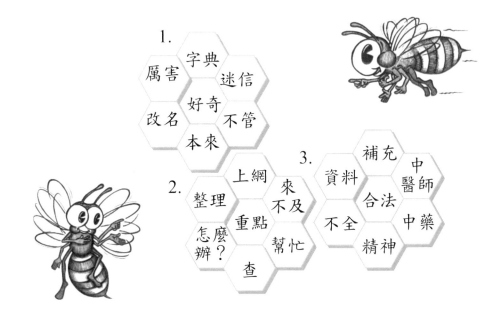

1. 字典　厲害　迷信　好奇　改名　不管　本來

2. 上網　整理　來不及　重點　怎麼辦？　幫忙　查

3. 補充　資料　中醫師　合法　不全　中藥　精神

→請用以上的字詞，說一個故事。

例1.　　有一天蜜蜜去找蜂蜂玩，蜂蜂正在查字典，蜜蜜很
　　　　好奇地問：「你為什麼寫了那麼多的鋒、峰、蜂字？」

　　　蜂蜂：「因為我想改名字。用金字邊的鋒，我就可以
　　　　　　變成很厲害的先鋒。用山字旁的峰，我就可以
　　　　　　像是很高大的山峰，不管用哪個字，都要比現
　　　　　　在這個小蟲子的蜂好。」

　　　蜜蜜：「我們本來就是蟲啊！事在人為，
　　　　　　別再迷信了！」

（2）看圖說故事

1. 男人對喝下午茶、吃甜點，一點興趣都沒有。
2. 水果開花！真的？假的？ 那是不可能的事。
3. 在台灣什麼都可以「補」，補洞、補牙，還可以補身體！
4. 他從早忙到晚，又吃得像鳥一樣少，請教醫師該補充什麼維他命？
5. 除了早餐吃好、中餐吃飽之外，還要晚餐吃得少，才是健康飲食。

【七·简体对话】

（1）去补习

小文： 对不起，我今天晚上要补习，不能跟你们出去玩了。

欧福： 你已经是大学生了，为什么还要去补习？

德美： 因为她要考研究所。

得中： 考研究所不能自己准备吗？

小文： 当然可以，只是我比较懒，去补习班，老师会帮我们整理重点。

德美： 小文，你一点都不懒！

得中： 就是啊！白天上课，晚上还要去补习班。

欧福： 对我们来说，那是不可能的事情！

小文： 我们已经习惯了，从小补到大。我得走了，拜拜！

（2）补一补

得中： 昨天听小文说「从小补到大」，我们不太懂意思，就上网查资料。

老师： 你们查到了什么资料？

德美： 好多！像是补课、补考、补票、补洞、补交作业、补充水份，这些　都好懂。

得中： 可是对补一补、吃补、补血、补气、补身体，就不太清楚了。

老师： 基本上「补」有「完、好」的意思，如果有不够、不全的情形，就需要补全它。

德美： 为什么要「从小补到大」呢？

老师： 因为人从小时候到大，应该说「到老」，身体如果缺少了什么？医师会建议吃不同的维他命。我们中医就会建议除了药补之外，还要食补。

得中： 哦！所以精神不好，就要喝鸡精补充精力，是吗？

老师： 学得真快！看来今天下午可以不用补课了！

DÌ JIǓ KÈ　　BǓ BǓ BǓ

（1）Qù Bǔxí

Xiǎowén: Duìbùqǐ, wǒ jīntiān wǎnshàng yào bǔxí, bùnéng gēn nǐmen chūqù wán le.

Ōufú: Nǐ yǐjīng shì dàxué shēng le, wèishéme háiyào qù bǔxí?

Déměi: Yīnwèi tā yào kǎo yánjiùsuǒ.

Dézhōng: Kǎo yánjiùsuǒ bùnéng zìjǐ zhǔnbèi ma?

Xiǎowén: Dāngrán kěyǐ, zhǐshì wǒ bǐjiào lǎn, qù bǔxíbān, Lǎoshī huì bāng wǒmen zhěnglǐ zhòngdiǎn.

Déměi: Xiǎowén, nǐ yìdiǎn dōu bù lǎn!

Dézhōng: Jiù shì ā! Báitiān shàngkè, wǎnshàng háiyào qù bǔxí bān.

Ōufú: Duì wǒmen lái shuō, nà shì bù kěnéng de shìqíng!

Xiǎowén: Wǒmen yǐjīng xíguàn le, cóng xiǎo bǔ dào dà. Wǒ děi zǒu le, bāibāi!

（2）Bǔ Yì Bǔ

Dézhōng: Zuótiān tīng Xiǎowén shuō "Cóng xiǎo bǔ dào dà", wǒmén bú tài dǒng yìsi, jiù shàngwǎng chá zīliào .

Lǎoshī: Nǐmén chá dào le shéme zīliào?

Déměi: Hǎoduō! Xiàng shì bǔkè、 bǔkǎo、 bǔpiào、 bǔdòng、bǔjiāo zuòyè、 bǔchōng shuǐfèn, zhèxiē dōu hǎo dǒng.

Dézhōng: Kěshì duì bǔ yì bǔ、 chībǔ、 bǔxiě、 bǔqì、 bǔ shēntǐ, jiù bú tài qīngchǔ le.

Lǎoshī: Jīběn shàng "Bǔ" yǒu "Wán、hǎo" de yìsi, rúguǒ yǒu búgòu、 bùquán de qíngxíng, jiù xūyào bǔquán tā 。

Déměi: Wèishéme yào "Cóng xiǎo bǔ dào dà" ne?

Lǎoshī: Yīnwèi rén cóng xiǎoshíhòu dào dà, yīnggāi shuō "dào lǎo", shēntǐ rúguǒ quēshǎo le shéme? Yīshī huì jiànyì chī bùtóng de wéitāmìng. Wǒmén zhōngyī jiù huì jiànyì chú le yàobǔ zhīwài, háiyào shíbǔ.

Dézhōng: Ō! Suǒyǐ jīngshén bùhǎo, jiùyào hē jījīng bǔchōng jīnglì, shìmā?

Lǎoshī: Xué de zhēn kuài! Kànlái jīntiān xiàwǔ kěyǐ búyòng bǔkè le!

【九 · 英文翻譯】

◆ **Dialogue** – p. 118~119

(1) Having Supplementary Classes

Xiaowen: I'm sorry, I have to go to a "buxiban", or supplementary school this evening, so I won't be able to go out with you.

Oufu: You're already a university student, why do you need supplemental classes?

Demei: Because she wants to study in graduate school.

Dezhong: Can't you prepare for graduate studies on your own?

Xiaowen: Of course I could, but I'm a little lazy, so by going to a "buxiban", the teacher can help me by providing study guidelines.

Demei: Xiaowen, you aren't lazy!

Dezhong: Yeah, really! Going to classes in the daytime and to "buxiban" in the evening.

Oufu: As for us, that would just be impossible!

Xiaowen: Oh, we're already used to it, "cramming" from childhood to adulthood. Well, I have to go now. Bye!

(2) Filling a Need

Dezhong: Yesterday I heard Xiaowen say, "Cong xiao bu dao da." We don't quite understand what that means, so we got on line to look it up.

Teacher: What did you find out?

Demei: A lot! For example, "make up a class", "make up a test", "to pay for a ticket after getting on the train", "to fill up a hole", "hand in homework late", and "to drink more water to prevent dehydration". These were easy to understand.

Dezhong: But as for "filling a need", "eat something nutritious", "nourishing the blood", "to nourish or conserve one's vitality", or "nourishing one's health", we don't understand those very clearly.

Teacher: Basically, "bu" has the meanings of "complete" and "well". If there isn't enough of something, or it is incomplete, then we need to make up the lack.

Demei: Then why do you need to "bu" from since you were a baby?

Teacher: Because from the time we are small until we are fully grown, or I should say, until we are old, what happens to our health if we are lacking something? The doctor will suggest that we take different vitamins. Our Chinese herb doctors would suggest that, in addition to medicine, we also need to eat certain kinds of nourishing foods.

Dezhong: Oh! Therefore, if someone lacks stamina, they should drink essence of chicken broth to increase their energy, right?

Teacher: You learn quickly! Looks like we won't have to "bu" the class this afternoon!

◆ Vocabulary – p. 120~121

1. graduate school — When I was in graduate school, I had already started working.
2. lazy — You are too lazy, sleeping until noon!
3. organize, arrange, tidy — We should tidy our rooms each day.
4. an important point — Hurry up and get to the important point.
5. just now — I have just bought a map.
6. education — Supplementary education is very common/ popular in Asia.
7. "cram", to do supplemental studies — Not only students, but adults as well go to "buxibans" for supplementary education.

8.	get on the Internet	Nowadays, university students spend more time on the Internet than they do talking.
9.	incomplete	The basic information you have given me is incomplete. Please turn in the rest of it tomorrow.
10.	information	Can I turn in the rest of the information tomorrow?
11.	water content, moisture	When mountain climbing, you need to drink water frequently to prevent dehydration.
12.	essentially, basically	Our ways of thinking are fundamentally the same.
13.	to make up a deficiency, to replenish	Is there anyone who wants to add something to the explanation?
14.	look up, check	Which web site did you look it up on?
15.	essence of chicken broth	When you lack stamina, does essence of chicken broth help?
16.	lack	Please tell me what other information is lacking.
17.	spirits, energy	Your spirits today are a lot better than they were yesterday.
18.	vitamin	People who do not like outdoor activities often lack vitamin D.
19.	physician	You should consult with a doctor, and not "self medicate".

◆ Grammar – p. 122

(1) Q: Do you want to go?
   A: Not even a little bit.
   1. Do you want to try it?
   2. Are you interested?
   3. Do you know?

(2) Q: How do you feel about six a.m.?
   A: As far as most people are concerned, that is just an impossible time.
   1. Students don't do their homework / teacher accept, acceptable
   2. Kids don't go to school?   Parents / agree

3. Fifty percent discount?   Boss/ business

(3) Q: What do you want to emphasize in your studies?
    A: In addition to improving my conversational abilities, I also want to learn calligraphy.

1. Why did you come to Taiwan?
2. Why do you want to take supplements?
3. What is your purpose in traveling abroad?

(4) Q: Why isn't he here yet?   **A:** It looks like he's not going to come today.

1. The wind and rain are so strong!   Is it a typhoon?
2. He is so happy!   Did he pass the test?
3. Why isn't the teacher talking?

◆ Word to Sentence – p. 123

1 補	to fill in, to be full	Hurry up and fill in this hole!
	to eat nutritious food, drink tonics	In times past, older people had the custom of eating special nutritious food in the winter.
	supplemental medicine	This is supplemental medicine for the patient.
	supplemental studies	Nowadays, almost every high school student goes to cram schools for supplemental courses after school.

Recently you've been so busy and have frequently gotten sick.　Perhaps it's because you go to school all day, and in the evening go to cram schools for supplemental education.　This has ruined your health.　I have heard that winter is the ideal time to drink tonics, so I have just gone to the Chinese herb doctor to buy you some supplemental medicine.

2 教	tutor, tutoring, family upbringing	"Family education" has the meaning of both "upbringing" and "private tutor".
	religion	Freedom of religion is everyone's right.

	classroom	This classroom's space and light are very good.
	to teach	Teaching is a very good career.

His parents are both educators so the family upbringing has been strict, with rules such as, "After class, you must stay in the classroom until all your homework has been finished, then you can come home." Also, he must read religious material for half an hour every day.

3 好	to say hello, to ask after	Please say "hello" to your family for me.
	hobby	My hobbies are mountain climbing and listening to music.
	good intention(s)	His intentions were good, so don't be angry with him.
	good deed(s), good thing	This is a good deed, so of course I am willing to help.

When you go back home to the countryside, please give my regards to your parents. I recall that your father doesn't have any hobbies, and just likes drinking alcohol. As a matter of fact, drinking a little each day is a good thing, as long as one doesn't drink to excess. My intentions in saying this are good, so ask him not to be angry with me!

第十課　三代同堂

【一‧對話】

（1）成家立業

德美： 老師，你住在哪裡？

老師： 我住在市區，跟我先生的父母住在一起。

得中： <u>老師看起來很年輕</u>，已經結婚了呀！

老師： 是啊！我還有兩個小孩子，一男一女。

歐福： 在台灣，結婚以後還跟父母住在一起嗎？

老師： <u>不一定，要看情形</u>，結婚以後住在一起的還不少。

得中： 中國人說「成家立業」，為什麼不成立自己的家呢？

老師： 嗯！這個成語用得真好。那是因為剛結婚沒什麼錢，
　　　 住在一起，可以省一點錢，慢慢存錢買自己的房子。

歐福　 哦！<u>存夠了錢，買了房子，就可以成家了。</u>

老師　 對！也有的是因為要照顧年老的父母。同時，祖父祖
　　　 母或是外公外婆，也可以幫忙照顧小孫子。

（2）越多越好

德美：　現代的父母，大概都是兩個人出去工作。

得中：　小孩子就需要有人照顧。

歐福：　那就對啦！花錢找保母，還不如請自己的父母帶孫子。

老師：　祖父母喜歡帶孫子，爸媽也放心，小孩子更高興。

德美：　嗯！這聽起來真的不錯，三代都可以互相幫忙。

得中：　一個家祖父、祖母、爸爸、媽媽，加上小孩子，人不會太多嗎？

老師：　還好吧！三代同堂是很幸福的。

歐福：　別忘了，中國人的觀念是越多越好！

德美：　對，他們喜歡熱鬧！

	生詞	簡體字	詞類	拼音	英譯
1.	年輕	年轻	Adj.	niánqīng	young
2.	結婚	结婚	V.	jiéhūn	marry
3.	成家立業	成家立业	V.	chéngjiā lìyè	establish a home and start a career
4.	成立	成立	V.	chénglì	establish
5.	成語	成语	N.	chéngyǔ	idiom
6.	省錢	省钱	V.	shěngqián	be(ing) thrifty
7.	存錢	存钱	V.	cúnqián	save money
8.	照顧	照顾	V.	zhàogù	take care of
9.	同時	同时	Adv.	tóngshí	at the same time
10.	現代	现代	N.	xiàndài	modern
11.	大概	大概	Adv.	dàgài	probably
12.	保母	保母	N.	bǎomǔ	baby sitter
13.	三代	三代	N.	sāndài	three generations
14.	互相	互相	Adv.	hùxiāng	mutual
15.	三代同堂	三代同堂	V.	sāndài tóngtáng	three generations living together
16.	幸福	幸福	Adj.	xìngfú	happiness, blessing
17.	觀念	观念	N.	guānniàn	concept, idea

【三‧生詞用法】

請填入適當的生詞

1. 省電、省水、_____都是我們應該做的。

2. _____人跟年紀大一點的人，想法差很多。

3. _____要用對，才不會鬧出笑話。

4. 這個公司_____多久了？

5. 每個人長大以後，都會想_____，有一個自己的家。

6. 我們已經_____二十多年了，覺得還是跟新婚一樣。

7. 古代跟_____的父母，對孩子的教養是很不同的。

8. 上一代的人傳給我們，我們再傳給下一代，____相傳。

9. 我不能_____做兩個事情，我要專心一點。

10. 人生病的時候，特別需要別人的_____。

11. 你們_____都知道怎麼去了吧？

12. 老人家不太容易接受新_____。

13. 愛人跟被愛都是一種很_____的感覺。

14. 我們是鄰居，當然應該_____幫忙。

15. 零存整付是一種很好的_____方法。

16. 祖孫三代住在一起，就是_____。

17. 現代的父母，大概要花五分之一的收入請_____。

【四‧語法】

(1) …看起來…

問：你覺得她怎麼樣？
答：她看起來很懂事。

   1. 錶？   看／很貴重
   2. 事情？ 聽／很複雜
   3. 東西？ 用／很順手

(2) 不一定，要看…

問：每一個學生都不喜歡做功課嗎？
答：不一定，要看是什麼功課。

   1. 父母答應？ 心情
   2. 老師有空？ 時間
   3. 朋友幫忙？ 事情

(3) …了…，…了…，就可以…了。

問：你打算什麼時候出國念書？
答：畢了業，存夠了錢，就可以出國念書了。

   1. 回國？
   2. 買船？
   3. 環遊世界？

(4) …，還不如…

問：要不要找人幫忙？
答：找人幫忙，還不如自己做。

   1. 訂做？
   2. 出去吃飯？
   3. 丟掉算了？

【五‧漢字】

1. 　　2. 　　3.

字⇨　詞⇨　句⇨　文

1 看	看看	不要這麼快做決定，再**看看**吧！
	偷看	自己寫自己的，不要**偷看**別人的。
	看上	我昨天**看上**了一件衣服，今天想去買。
	看輕	別**看輕**那個年輕人，他是明日之星。

　　國王跟公主說：今天的舞會上，會有很多的王子來，你先**偷看**一下，告訴父王，你**看上**了誰，我們再來**看看**他的背景，別**看輕**那些小個子的王子喔！他們人雖然長得不高，可能志氣卻是很高的。

2 如	比如	**比如**說毛巾、牙刷，都是「日常用品」。
	不如	送他禮物**不如**送他錢有用。
	如意	每個人都希望人生是順利**如意**的。
	如果	**如果**沒事的話，我想先走了。

　　如果碰到不**如意**的事情，不要單獨一個人坐在家裡哭，**不如**找個朋友聊聊，出去走走。**比如**說，去爬爬山，到海邊沙灘去走走，讓風吹走那些不**如意**的事情。

3 省	節省	冷氣開小一點，再開電扇，可以**節省**電力。
	反省	從小到大，父母就常常要我們**反省**。
	省事	花錢請人來做，比較**省事**。
	省錢	為了**省錢**，找這麼多麻煩，真不值得！

　　姊姊對弟弟說：「你看我們的父母那麼**節省**，一點都不浪費，我們也應該**反省**一下，可以怎麼**省錢**？」弟弟說：「我的學校很近，我可以自己走路上學，不必爸媽接送，**省事**又**省錢**！」

【六·練習】

(1) 填入適當用詞

我們很像，可是我們不一樣：

1. 你___快去吧！
2. 他打你，你___跟他玩嗎？
3. 會說中文的人___。
4. 家裡___現金嗎？
5. 今天公司的事情___。
6. 怎麼了？你___嗎？
7. ___什麼事嗎？
8. 一動___一靜。
9. 他不但有錢，___房子。
10. 這個事情___要跟他說清楚。
11. 出去玩___在家聽音樂。
12. 你已經有很多玩具了，___買嗎？

> A.還有
> B.還是
> C.還要
> D.還好
> E.還不如
> F.還不少

我更不一樣 ── 認識破音字：

1. 這是定價，不能___了。
2. 俗話說：___、再借不難。
3. 聖經上說：___、以眼還眼。
4. 這個教室用完了，一定要把桌椅___。
5. 我不能收這麼貴重的禮物，請你___給他。

> A.還原
> B.退還
> C.有借有還
> D.討價還價
> E.以牙還牙

(2) 數來寶 ─ 見面要問好：

見面要問好！
見到師長要問好！
怎麼問？
欠欠身 彎彎腰 點點頭 笑一笑
當然最好開口叫
怎麼叫？
長輩跟著朋友叫
爺爺 奶奶 阿公 阿嬤 阿姨 叔叔
再加一個「好」
老師的先生叫師丈
老師的太太叫師母
平輩點點頭
小輩說你好
進門要問好！
早上說「早」
白天說「你好」
晚上見面說「你好」
晚上再見說「晚安」
有禮人見人愛
無禮沒人愛
失禮更是大阻礙

(3)看圖說故事

馮超 攝

1. 出去吃飯，還不如自己動手做。
2. 媽媽現在照顧你，等你大了就自由了。
3. 照顧老人家身體同時也要顧到他的精神。
4. 他們的語言不同，但是關係很好，看起來很舒服。
5. 年輕人結了婚，有了孩子，當然就是成家立業了。

（1）成家立业

德美： 老师，你住在哪里？

老师： 我住在市区，跟我先生的父母住在一起。

得中： <u>老师看起来很年轻</u>，已经结婚了呀！

老师： 是啊！我还有两个小孩子，一男一女。

欧福： 在台湾，结婚以后还跟父母住在一起吗？

老师： <u>不一定，要看情形</u>，结婚以后住在一起的还不少。

得中： 中国人说「成家立业」，为什么不成立自己的家呢？

老师： 嗯！这个成语用得真好。那是因为刚结婚没什么钱，
住在一起，可以省一点钱，慢慢存钱买自己的房子。

欧福 哦！<u>存够了钱，买了房子，就可以成家了。</u>

老师 对！也有的是因为要照顾年老的父母。同时，祖父祖
母或是外公外婆，也可以帮忙照顾小孙子。

（2）越多越好

德美： 现代的父母，大概都是两个人出去工作。

得中： 小孩子就需要有人照顾。

欧福： 那就对啦！<u>花钱找保母，还不如请自己的父母带孙子。</u>

老师： 祖父母喜欢带孙子，爸妈也放心，小孩子更高兴。

德美： 嗯！这听起来真的不错，三代都可以互相帮忙。

得中： 一个家祖父、祖母、爸爸、妈妈，加上小孩子，人不
会太多吗？

老师： 还好吧！三代同堂是很幸福的。

欧福： 别忘了，中国人的观念是越多越好！

德美： 对，他们喜欢热闹！

【八‧拼音對照】

DÌ SHÍ KÈ　　SĀNDÀI TÓNG TÁNG

（1） Chéngjiā Lìyè

Déměi: 　Lǎoshī, nǐ zhù zài nǎlǐ?

Lǎoshī: 　Wǒ zhù zài shìqū, gēn wǒ xiānsheng de fùmǔ zhù zài

yìqǐ.

Dézhōng: Lǎoshī kàn qǐlái hěn niánqīng, yǐjīng jiéhūn le ya!

Lǎoshī: Shì a ! Wǒ háiyǒu liǎngge xiǎo háizi, yì nán yì nǚ.

Ōufú: Zài Táiwān, jiéhūn yǐhòu háiyào gēn fùmǔ zhù zài yìqǐ ma?

Lǎoshī: Bù yídìng, yào kàn qíngxíng, jiéhūn yǐhòu zhù zài yìqǐ de hái bùshǎo.

Dézhōng: Zhōngguó rén shuō "chéngjiā lìyè", wèishéme bù chénglì zìjǐ de jiā ne ?

Lǎoshī: En! Zhèige chéngyǔ yòng de zhēn hǎo. Nà shì yīnwèi gāng jiéhūn méi shéme qián, zhù zài yìqǐ, kěyǐ shěng yìdiǎn qián, mànmàn cúnqián mǎi zìjǐ de fángzi.

Ōufú: O! Cún gòule qián, mǎile fángzi, jiù kěyǐ chéngjiā le.

Lǎoshī: Duì! Yě yǒude shì yīnwèi yào zhàogù niánlǎo de fùmǔ. Tóngshí, zǔfù zǔmǔ huòshì wàigōng wàipó, yě kěyǐ bāngmáng zhàogù xiǎo sūnzi.

(2) Yuè Duō Yuè Hǎo

Déměi: Xiàndài de fùmǔ, dàgài dōushì liǎngge rén chūqù gōngzuò.

Dézhōng: Xiǎoháizi jiù xūyào yǒu rén zhàogù.

Ōufú: Nà jiù duì la! Huāqián zhǎo bǎomǔ, hái bùrú qǐng zìjǐ de fùmǔ dài sūnzi.

Lǎoshī: Zǔfùmǔ xǐhuān dài sūnzi, bàmā yě fàngxīn, xiǎoháizi gèng gāoxìng.

Déměi: En! Zhè tīng qǐlái zhēnde búcuò, sāndài dōu kěyǐ hùxiāng bāngmáng.

Dézhōng: Yíge jiā zǔfù, zǔmǔ, bàba, māma, jiāshàng xiǎoháizi, rén búhuì tài duō ma?

Lǎoshī: Háihǎo ba! Sāndài tóngtáng shì hěn xìngfú de.

Ōufú: Bié wàngle, Zhōngguó rén de guānniàn shì yuè duō yuè hǎo!

Déměi: Duì, tāmen xǐhuān rènào!

【九・英文翻譯】

◆ **Dialogue** – p. 133~134

(1) Family and Career

Demei: Teacher, where do you live?

Teacher: I live downtown, with my husband's parents.

Dezhong: Teacher, you look so young, and you're already married!

Teacher: That's right! I also have two children – a boy and a girl.

Oufu: In Taiwan, people still live with their parents after getting married?

Teacher: It depends on the situation, but quite a few people do.

Dezhong: Chinese people say, "Establish a family and start a career." Why not start your own family?

Teacher: Hmm. You've quoted an appropriate idiom. We do live together, because when you first get married you don't have much money, so this way we can gradually save up to buy our own house.

Oufu: Oh! Save enough money, buy a house and then establish a family.

Teacher: Right! Another reason is to take care of aged parents. At the same time, the grandparents can also take care of their grandchildren.

(2) The More the Better

Demei: Most modern parents are both working people.

Dezhong: Children need someone to take care of them.

Oufu: That's right! Spending money on baby sitters isn't as good as asking your own parents to watch their grandchildren.

Teacher: Grandparents enjoy taking care of their grandchildren, the parents can put their minds at ease, and the children are happy.

Demei: Hmm! That sounds pretty good. The three generations can help each other.

Dezhong: With a family made up of grandparents, parents, and children, isn't that too crowded?.

Teacher: It's okay! Three generations living together is a great happiness for us.

Oufu: Don't forget, Chinese people think, "The more, the better."

Demei: Right, they like "hubbub"!

◆ Vocabulary – p. 135

1. be(ing) thrifty   Conserving electricity, conserving water, and being thrifty are what we should do.

2. young   The way young people and older people think have some differences.

3. idiom   Idioms must be used correctly, or you will get laughed at.

4. establish   How long has this company been established?

5. establish a home and start a career   Everybody wants to establish a home and start a career after they grow up.

6. marry   We've already been married more than twenty years, but still feel like newlyweds.

7. modern   Ancient and modern parents have very different ideas about how to raise children.

8. three generations   The previous generation passed a legacy on to us, and we pass it on to the next generation, so three generations carry on the legacy.

9. at the same time   I cannot do two things at once, I need to concentrate.

10. take care of   When someone gets sick, they really need somebody to take care of them.

11. probably   You probably all know how to go, don't you?

12. concept, idea   Older people cannot easily accept new ideas.

13. happiness, blessing   Loving others and being loved in return is a great happiness and blessing.

14. mutual   We are neighbors, so of course we should help each other.

15. save money   A good way to save money is to accumulate small amounts over a long period of time.

16. three generations living together   Grandparents, parents and grandchildren living together is "San dai tong tang".

17. baby sitter   Modern parents probably have to spend one fifth of
                          their income on child care.

◆ Grammar – p. 137

(1) ...looks like... / ...resembles...
Q: What do you think of her?
A: She looks likes a sophisticated person.
 1. Watch?   looks / very expensive
 2. Business?   sound (like) / very complicated
 3. That?   use / very handily

(2) ...that depends on (the situation)...
Q: Does every student dislike doing homework?
A: That depends on what kind of homework it is.
 1. Parents agree / mood
 2. Teacher to have spare time / time
 3. Friends help / matter, business

(3) After...are completed, then (you) can...
Q: When do you plan to go abroad to study?
A: After graduating, and saving enough money, then I can go abroad to
    study.
 1. return to one's own country
 2. buying a yacht
 3. travel the world

(4) ...not as good as...
Q: Do you want to find someone to help you?
A: Looking for someone to help is not as good as doing it yourself.
 1. order specially
 2. go out to eat
 3. throw away

◆ Word to Sentence – p. 137

1 看	take a look	Do not decide so quickly, and take another look!
	peek at, observe secretly	Do your own writing, and do not peek at others' work.
	to have one's eyes on	Yesterday I had my eye on a piece of clothing, and today I'd like to buy it.
	underestimate, look down on	Do not look down on that young man.　He is one of the shining stars of the future.

　The king said to the princess, "At today's ball, there will be a lot of princes.　You can observe them secretly and tell me which one you have your eye on.　Then we will look into his background.　Also, do not look down on any short princes, because even though they may not be very tall, their ambition could be great.

2 如	for example	We can say, for example, that towels and toothbrushes are "items for daily use".
	not as good as	Sending him a present is not as good or as useful as sending him money.
	as one likes, without impediments	Everybody hopes that their lives can go smoothly.
	if, supposing	If there's nothing else, I think I'll leave now.

　If one encounters obstacles and impediments, sitting alone at home and crying isn't nearly as good as finding a friend to talk with, or going out for a walk.　For example, one can climb a mountain, or go walking along the beach, and let the breezes blow all your cares away.

3 省	to save, conserve	If we set the air conditioner at a higher temperature and use a fan with it, we can save electricity.
	to self- reflect, meditate	Since childhood, my parents have asked me to engage in introspection.
	to avoid trouble or extra work	Spending money to ask someone to come in and do this work will avoid going to extra trouble and effort.

to save money	Going to all this trouble and effort to save money is really not worth it!

Elder sister says to younger brother, "Look at how our parents like to conserve, and not waste anything. We really should think deeply about this, and see if we can somehow save money." Younger brother says, "My school is pretty close by, so I could walk to school myself, and it wouldn't be necessary for Mom and Dad to send me or pick me up. That would save effort and money!"

◆ Practice –

(1) p. 138 Fill in the Blanks.
We are Similar but We are Different.

(2) p.139 Chant ― Greet Someone When You Meet Them
Listen to the teacher, and repeat each line three times. After becoming familiar with the rthythm, move on to the next section of the chant.

Greet someone when you meet them,
Greet the teacher and older people when you meet them.
How?
Bow slightly, bow deeply, nod your head, smile.
Best of all, say something in greeting.
How?
For older people, just repeat what you hear your friends call them.
"Grandfather", "Grandmother", "Grandpa", "Grandma", "Aunt",
"Uncle",
Then add a "hao" at the end!
Teacher's husband is called "Shi zhang".
Teacher's wife is called "Shi mu".
Among friends just nod your head,
For younger people just say "Ni hao."
When you enter a room, greet the people in it.
In the morning, say "Zao."
In the daytime, say "Ni hao."
When meeting someone in the evening say "Ni hao."
When you part in the evening, say "Wan an."
Everybody will love you when you are courteous;
No one will love when you're not!
Rudeness is a big obstacle in your social life.

第十一課　傳統與現代

【一・對話】

（1）超級市場

德美：　老師你平常在哪裡買菜？

老師：　我喜歡去傳統市場買菜。

得中：　老師家附近沒有超級市場嗎？

老師：　有是有，可是我還是習慣在傳統市場買。那裡的東西
　　　　比較新鮮、便宜，而且有很多選擇。

德美：　話是沒錯，可是我覺得超級市場比傳統市場乾淨。

得中：　我也這麼覺得。在我的國家雖然也有傳統市場，但是
　　　　還是有很多人喜歡去超級市場買菜。

老師：　我喜歡去傳統市場買菜，還有一個最大的原因，就是
　　　　那裡可以討價還價，超級市場就不行了。

（2）傳統市場

德美： 台灣的傳統市場一大早就那麼熱鬧啊！

老師： 走，我帶你們去幾個又新鮮又便宜的攤子。

得中： 老師你剛剛討價還價，買了三樣水果不到一百塊，真
　　　 便宜！

德美： 那位賣水果的老闆好像認識老師。

老師： 是啊！我常常來這裡買水果。只要你講價，老闆就一
　　　 定算你便宜。

得中： 傳統市場好像比超級市場有人情味多了。超級市場的
　　　 工作人員常常換，大家各忙各的，沒人理你。

德美： 以後我們應該常到傳統市場買菜，一方面可以殺價，
　　　 一方面可以練習中文。

【 二 · 生詞 】

	生詞	簡體字	詞類	拼音	英譯
1.	平常	平常	Adj.	píngcháng	usually, commonly
2.	傳統市場	传统市场	N.	chuántǒng shìchǎng	traditional market
3.	超級市場	超级市场	N.	chāojí shìchǎng	supermarket
4.	新鮮	新鲜	Adj.	xīnxiān	fresh
5.	而且	而且	Conj.	érqiě	and also
6.	選擇	选择	N. V.	xuǎnzé	choice, selection
7.	話是沒錯	话是没错	Adj.	huà shì méicuò	You said it!
8.	乾淨	干净	Adj.	gānjìng	clean
9.	大部分	大部分	Adj.	dàbùfèn	most
10.	原因	原因	N.	yuányīn	reason
11.	討價還價	讨价还价	V.	tǎojià huánjià	haggle over the price
12.	一大早	一大早	Adj.	yídàzǎo	early in the morning
13.	攤子	摊子	N.	tānzi	stand
14.	講價	讲价	V.	jiǎngjià	bargain
15.	算	算	V.	suàn	calculate
16.	人情味	人情味	N.	rénqíng wèi	warm human relations
17.	各忙各的	各忙各的	Adj.	gèmáng gède	everybody busy with their own affairs
18.	不理	不理	V.	bùlǐ	ignore

【三‧生詞用法】

請填入適當的生詞

1. 這附近的傳統市場東西多，_____很新鮮。

2. 有的_____開放二十四小時，非常方便。

3. 我_____不喝咖啡，考試的時候才喝。

4. 這條魚又_____又便宜，不買可惜。

5. 媽媽說手不_____不可以吃飯。

6. 在都市裡，_____越來越少了。

7. A：貴的東西不一定好。

　　B：_____。可是便宜的東西容易壞。

8. 這裡只有一家西餐廳，沒有別的_____。

9. 我跟我女朋友吵架了，她見到我都_____我。

10. 一大早學校附近就有許多賣早餐的_____。

11. 他昨天沒來上課的_____，你知道嗎？

12. _____的外國人沒有吃宵夜的習慣。

13. 鄉下比都市有_____多了。

14. 他_____就去學校上課了。

15. 台灣人買東西有_____的習慣。

16. 老闆年紀大了，常常_____錯錢。

17. 在台灣買東西，不是什麼地方都能_____。

18. 在德國我有很多朋友，可是大家_____很少見面。

【四‧語法】

（1）…，而且…

問：你媽媽是老師嗎？
答：我媽媽是老師，而且還是一位好老師。

    1.你的女朋友漂亮嗎？   很漂亮／很聰明
    2.那家店的飲料多不多？   很多／很好喝
    3.那裡的風景美嗎？   很美／可愛的猴子

（2）話是沒錯，可是…。

A：我覺得在超級市場買菜比較好。
B：話是沒錯，可是我還是習慣在傳統市場買。

    1.A：我覺得今天的考試太難了。 B：太簡單／沒意思
    2.A：你應該少喝咖啡，早一點睡覺。 B：習慣／三杯
    3.A：你應該早一點來。 B：剛才／知道

（3）…比…多了。

例：超級市場比傳統市場乾淨多了。

    1.他寫的字怎麼樣？
    2.那家餐廳的菜怎麼樣？
    3.這部電視怎麼樣？

（4）…，一方面…，一方面…。

例：去傳統市場買菜，一方面可以講價，一方面可以學中文。

    1.夏天去百貨公司，可以吹冷氣／可以逛街
    2.喝無糖飲料，對身體好／可以減肥
    3.我上個月去日本，去旅行／去看朋友

【五・漢字】

1.   2.   3.

字⇨ 詞⇨ 句⇨ 文

1 習	學習	活到老學到老，是最好的**學習**態度。
	複習	課前預習，課後**複習**，是最好的學習方法。
	習題	做完了**習題**，你幫我看看，好不好？
	習慣	我有吃完飯吃甜點的**習慣**。

    老師經常說：「課前預習，課後**複習**。」所以，我從小就有那樣的讀書**習慣**，當天的**習題**一定當天做完，再先預習一下明天的功課，我覺得那是一種最好的**學習**方法。

2 價	講價	「**講價**」就是請賣方算便宜一點。
	原價	我們講的價錢是**原價**的一半。
	價錢	這個**價錢**太不合理了，一定要殺價。
	價格	這是公訂的**價格**，我沒辦法算你便宜。

    老闆說他賣我的**價錢**已經是市場**價格**的一半了，我看了**原價**的牌子，那是真的，他沒騙我，所以我就沒再跟他**講價**錢了。

3 趣	有趣	我在酒館看到一個很**有趣**的事情。
	興趣	看書是我的嗜好，寫作是我的**興趣**。
	趣事	旅行的時候，發生了很多**趣事**。
	趣味	這兩張畫有不同的**趣味**。

    這件事情真是**有趣**，我們 37 年沒見了，談起以前中學時代發生的**趣事**，大家都還覺得很有**趣味**，談得很開心。我想那個時候，我們的**興趣**就很接近，所以雖然現在我們都是中年人了，還是很談得來。

【六‧練習】

（1）魔鏡

1. 　　　每個人都愛聽**故事**。
2. 　我親眼看見那個交通**事故**發生，好可怕！
3. 　　　　　**科學**是我最愛的學科。
4. 　我期中考試的三個**學科**都通過了。
5. 　　你知道圖書館**開放**的時間嗎？
6. 　　　　你**放開**我，讓我走！
7. 　我應該要好好**用功**讀書。
8. 新型的手機有很多種**功用**。
9. 　　　他是**好心**告訴你，不要生氣。
10. 　　　「**心好**」比什麼都重要。
11. 　明天的天氣會**好轉**嗎？
12. 等一下，等我把蓋子**轉好**再走。

(2)看圖說故事

蔡玲敏 攝

1. 畫畫比看報紙有意思多了。
2. 外國人看到中國式的傳統衣飾，忍不住想試試。
3. 這傳統小吃比那下午茶好吃多了，而且價錢也便宜多了。
4. 這不是簡單的工作，一方面得握住狗嘴巴，一方面得修剪狗毛。
5. 平常老人家愛住傳統式的房子，不愛住現代化的大樓。

（1）超级市场

德美： 老师你平常在哪里买菜？

老师： 我喜欢去传统市场买菜。

得中： 老师家附近没有超级市场吗？

老师： 有是有，可是我还是习惯在传统市场买。那里的东西比较新鲜、便宜，而且有很多选择。

德美： 话是没错，可是我觉得超级市场比传统市场干净。

得中： 我也这么觉得。在我的国家虽然也有传统市场，但是还是有很多人喜欢去超级市场买菜。

老师： 我喜欢去传统市场买菜，还有一个最大的原因，就是那里可以讨价还价，超级市场就不行了。

（2）传统市场

德美： 台湾的传统市场一大早就那么热闹啊！

老师： 走，我带你们去几个又新鲜又便宜的摊子。

得中： 老师你刚刚讨价还价，买了三样水果不到一百块，真便宜！

德美： 那位卖水果的老板好像认识老师。

老师： 是啊！我常常来这里买水果。只要你讲价，老板就一定算你便宜。

得中： 传统市场好像比超级市场有人情味多了。超级市场的工作人员常常换，大家各忙各的，没人理你。

德美： 以后我们应该常到传统市场买菜，一方面可以杀价，一方面可以练习中文。

DÌ SHÍ YĪ KÈ　　CHUÁNTǑNG YǓ XIÀNDÀI

（1）Chāojí Shìchǎng

Déměi：　Lǎoshī nǐ píngcháng zài nǎlǐ mǎi cài?

Lǎoshī：　Wǒ xǐhuān qù chuántǒng shìchǎng mǎi cài.

Dézhōng: Lǎoshī jiā fùjìn méiyǒu chāojí shìchǎng ma?

Lǎoshī: Yǒu shìyǒu, kěshì wǒ háishì xíguàn zài chuántǒng shìchǎng mǎi. Nàlǐ de dōngxi bǐjiào xīnxiān, piányí, érqiě yǒu hěnduō xuǎnzé.

Déměi: Huà shì méicuò, kěshì wǒ juéde chāojí shìchǎng bǐ chuántǒng shìchǎng gānjìng.

Dézhōng: Wǒ yě zhème juéde. Zài wǒde guójiā suīrán yě yǒu chuántǒng shìchǎng, dànshì háishì yǒu hěn duō rén xǐhuān qù chāojí shìchǎng mǎi cài.

Lǎoshī: Wǒ xǐhuān qù chuántǒng shìchǎng mǎi cài, háiyǒu yíge zuì dà de yuányīn, jiùshì nàlǐ kěyǐ tǎojià huánjià, chāojí shìchǎng jiù bùxíng le.

(2) Chuántǒng Shìchǎng.

Déměi: Táiwān de chuántǒng shìchǎng yídàzǎo jiù nàme rènào a!

Lǎoshī: Zǒu, wǒ dài nǐmen qù jǐge yòu xīnxiān yòu piányí de tānzi.

　　　　＊　　　＊　　　＊　　　＊　　　＊

Dézhōng: Lǎoshī nǐ gānggāng tǎojià huánjià, mǎile sānyàng shuǐguǒ búdào yìbǎikuài, zhēn piányí!

Déměi: Nàwèi mài shuǐguǒ de lǎobǎn hǎoxiàng rènshì Lǎoshī.

Lǎoshī: Shì a! Wǒ chángcháng lái zhèlǐ mǎi shuǐguǒ. Zhǐyào nǐ jiǎngjià, lǎobǎn jiù yídìng suàn nǐ piányí.

Dézhōng: Chuántǒng shìchǎng hǎoxiàng bǐ chāojí shìchǎng yǒu rénqíng wèi duō le. Chāojí shìchǎng de gōngzuò rényuán chángcháng huàn, dàjiā gè máng gè de, méi rén lǐ nǐ.

Déměi: Yǐ hòu wǒmen yīnggāi cháng dào chuántǒng shìchǎng mǎi cài, yì fāngmiàn kěyǐ shājià, yì fāngmiàn kěyǐ liànxí Zhōngwén.

◆ **Dialogue** – p. 148~149

(1) Supermarket

Demei: Teacher, where do you usually buy food?

Teacher: I like to shop in the traditional markets.

Dezhong: Don't you have a supermarket near your house?

Teacher: There is one, but I'm still more used to shopping in the traditional market. Things there are fresher and cheaper, and there's a large selection.

Demei: What you say is true, but I think the supermarket is cleaner than the traditional market.

Dezhong: I think so, too. Even though my country also has traditional markets, many people still prefer supermarkets.

Teacher: There is another good reason I like traditional markets, and that's the fact that I can bargain and talk the price down. You can't do that in a supermarket!

(2) Traditional Marketplaces.

Demei: Taiwan's traditional markets have so much activity so early in the morning!

Teacher: Let's go! Let me show you a few stands where the goods are fresh and cheap.

Dezhong: Teacher, you just haggled the price down, buying three different kinds of fruit for less than NT$100. That's cheap!

Demei: That fruit vendor seems to know the teacher.

Teacher: That's right. I often come here to buy fruit. If you bargain, the vendor will give you a discount.

Dezhong: Traditional markets seem friendlier and more personal than supermarkets. A supermarket's staff changes all the time, everybody is busy working, and no one pays attention to you.

Demei: Later on, we should come to the traditional market more often. That way, we can bargain and learn Chinese.

◆ Vocabulary – p. 150~151

1.	and also	This nearby traditional market's food has a wide selection and is also fresh.
2.	supermarket	Some supermarkets are open 24 hours, which is very convenient.
3.	usually, commonly	I don't usually drink coffee, only when I have tests.
4.	fresh	This fish is so fresh and so cheap, it would be a pity not to buy it!
5.	clean	Mom says, "If your hands are dirty you can't eat."
6.	traditional market	In cities, there are fewer and fewer traditional markets.
7.	You said it!	A: Expensive things are not necessarily good quality. B: You said it! But cheap things are easily broken.
8.	choice, selection	There is only one western restaurant here. There are no other choices.
9.	ignore	I argued with my girlfriend, and now she ignores me.
10.	stand	In the early morning, there are a lot of breakfast stands near the school.
11.	reason	Do you know the reason he didn't come to class yesterday?
12.	most	Most people from other countries do not have the custom of eating late night snacks.
13.	warm human relations	People in the countryside are friendlier than people in the city.
14.	early in the morning	He went to school in the early morning.
15.	haggle over the price	People in Taiwan have the custom of haggling when they buy things.
16.	calculate	The store owner is getting old, and frequently makes mistakes calculating the money.
17.	bargain	When you buy things in Taiwan, you cannot haggle over the price everywhere you shop.

18. everybody busy with their own affairs I have a lot of friends in Germany, but everybody is busy with their own affairs, so we seldom see each other.

◆ Grammar – p. 152

(1) ...and, also...

Q: Is your mother a teacher?

A: My mother is not only a teacher, but furthermore is a good teacher!

1. Is your girlfriend pretty?   pretty / smart
2. Does that shop have many kinds of drinks?   many / tasty
3. Is the scenery beautiful there?   very beautiful / cute monkeys

(2) What you say is true, but...

A： I think shopping in the supermarket is better.

B： I'm still more used to shopping at the traditional market.

1. A: I think today's test was too hard. B: If it's too easy it isn't interesting.
2. A: You should drink less coffee, and go to bed earlier.
   B: I'm used to drinking three cups a day.
3. A: You should have come earlier.   B: I just found out myself!

(3) ...compared to...better than / more than...

Example: Supermarkets are cleaner than traditional markets.

1. How well does he write Chinese characters?
2. How is the food in that restaurant?
3. How good is that television?

(4) ...on one hand...and / but on the other hand...

Example: Shopping in traditional markets is better because / you can bargain / you can learn Chinese.

1. Shopping in department stores in the summer is better because / you can enjoy the air conditioning / you can window shop
2. Drinking sugarless beverages is better because / it's good for your health / can also lose weight
3. I went to Japan last month because / I went sightseeing / I visited friends

◆ Word to Sentence – p. 153

1 習	study, learn	"One is never too old to learn." is the best attitude to have about studying.
	review	Previewing before the lesson, and reviewing after the lesson are the best methods of studying.
	exercise, homework	After I finish the exercise, could you look it over for me?
	custom, habit	I am in the habit of eating a dessert after my meals.

Teachers frequently say, "Preview before each lesson, and review afterwards." So, since childhood I have been in the habit of studying that way. I finish each day's homework exercises on that day, then I preview tomorrow's lesson. I feel that this is one of the very best methods of studying.

2 價	to haggle, to bargain	"Haggling" is when you ask the seller to give you a lower price.
	the original price	The price we are discussing is half the original cost.
	cost	The cost is too unreasonably high, so we have to talk the price down.
	price	This is the standard price set by the government, and there is no way I can sell it to you more cheaply.

The boss says that the price he is giving me is already half of the market price. Looking at the price tag, I can see that it's true and that he's not fooling me, so I will not haggle with him any further.

3 趣	interesting	I saw something interesting in a bar.
	interest, enthusiasm	Reading is my hobby, and I am interested in writing.
	amusing incident, interesting episode	Many amusing, interesting things happen while one is traveling.
	fun, interest, taste	These two pictures are interesting in different ways.

This was a very interesting experience. We hadn't seen each other for thirty-seven years, but when we met and talked about fun things that had happened in junior high, we still felt it was amusing and had a good time. I think back then we had very similar tastes and interests, so even though we're middle-aged now, we still have things to share and talk about.

第十二課　參觀社區

【一·對話】

(1) 辦公大樓

歐福：　台灣的大樓都好高！這些都是辦公室嗎？

老師：　不一定，有些是純辦公大樓，有些是綜合式的大樓。

德美：　什麼是綜合式的大樓？

得中：　我猜猜看。是不是有公司也有住家？

老師：　真聰明！一猜就猜中了。這些綜合式的大樓裡面有
　　　　辦公室、個人的工作室，也有住家。

德美：　那樣不是很複雜嗎？

老師：　的確很複雜，不認識也不知道鄰居是做什麼的。

歐福：　既然有純辦公大樓，那麼也有純住家大樓嗎？

老師：　有，那些純住家大樓，就單純多了。看！就像那樣
　　　　的新社區，跟剛才的比起來是不是好多了。

（2）舊社區

老師：　你們看這附近的房子，跟我們剛才看的有什麼不一
　　　　樣？

得中：　這一區的房子好像比較舊，也沒那麼高了。

老師：　這些就是比大樓更早期的公寓。

歐福：　除了新舊之外，還有什麼不同嗎?

老師：　公寓大多是五樓以下，沒有電梯，也沒有管理員。

德美：　哇！這一區的房子好漂亮啊！

老師：　這裡是新的獨門獨戶的別墅區。比比看！跟透天的房
　　　　子有什麼差別？

	生詞	簡體字	詞類	拼音	英譯
1.	純	纯	Adj.	chún	pure
2.	辦公	办公	V.	bàngōng	do office work
3.	綜合式	综合式	Adj.	zònghéshì	mixed style
4.	猜	猜	V.	cāi	to guess
5.	住家	住家	N.	zhùjiā	family residence
6.	聰明	聪明	Adj.	cōngmíng	smart, clever, intelligent
7.	工作室	工作室	N.	gōngzuòshì	studio
8.	複雜	复杂	Adj.	fùzá	complicated, complex
9.	的確	的确	Adj.	díquè	certain, sure
10.	鄰居	邻居	N.	línjū	neighbor
11.	既然	既然	Conj.	jìrán	since
12.	社區	社区	N.	shèqū	community, neighborhood
13.	附近	附近	N.	fùjìn	nearby
14.	早期	早期	Adj.	zǎoqí	early period
15.	電梯	电梯	N.	diàntī	elevator
16.	管理員	管理员	N.	guǎnlǐyuán	superintendent, janitor
17.	獨門獨戶	独门独户	Adj.	dúméndúhù	single family unit
18.	別墅	別墅	N.	biéshù	dacha
19.	透天	透天	Adj.	tòutiān	multi-storied house belonging to a single family
20.	差別	差别	N.	chābié	difference, discrepancy

【三‧生詞用法】

請填入適當的生詞

1. 這是綜合了辦公室跟＿＿＿＿＿＿的大樓。

2. 我們點一個＿＿＿＿＿＿的沙拉吧！

3. ＿＿＿＿＿＿反被＿＿＿＿＿誤。

4. 你＿＿＿＿＿看我幾歲？

5. 別想得太＿＿＿＿＿了！

6. 老師的＿＿＿＿＿室在哪裡？

7. 這是百分之百的＿＿＿＿＿果汁嗎？

8. 我想把這間公寓改變成＿＿＿＿＿。

9. 我們可以分租一棟四層樓＿＿＿＿＿的房子。

10. ＿＿＿＿＿你沒時間，我們就改天再談。

11. 那＿＿＿＿＿是一個很聰明的做法。

12. 我們去跟＿＿＿＿＿打一聲招呼吧！

13. 這兩種飲料有什麼＿＿＿＿＿？

14. 這＿＿＿＿＿有公寓出租嗎？

15. ＿＿＿＿＿的房子一定很貴。

16. 我們家在鄉下有一棟透天的＿＿＿＿＿。

17. 那是一個很安全又很安靜的＿＿＿＿＿。

18. 地震的時候不要坐＿＿＿＿＿。

19. ＿＿＿＿＿的電影是黑白片。

20. 這裡的＿＿＿＿＿要管很多的事情。

【四·語法】

(1) 比…更…

問：摩托車好騎嗎？　答：很好騎，比腳踏車更好騎。

1. 歐元的匯率高不高？
2. 現在的工作好找嗎？
3. 他適應國外的生活嗎？

(2) 既然…就…

問：你真的沒有別的女朋友嗎？
答：既然你問了，我就告訴你吧！

1. 買了／用
2. 沒空／別去了
3. 相信／別問他

(3) 跟…比起來

問：台灣的天氣怎麼樣？　答：跟德國比起來，熱多了！

1. 這台機器怎麼樣？　　　手工／方便多了
2. 這個小花園怎麼樣？　　公園／小多了
3. 昨天的功課怎麼樣？　　報告／輕鬆多了

(4) 除了…之外，還有…

問：你們家有幾輛車？　答：除了這輛車之外，還有一輛。

1. 我可以去哪裡領錢？　　　銀行／郵局
2. 飯後還有什麼？　　　　　咖啡／甜點
3. 你沒車，怎麼去學校？　　公車／捷運

【五‧漢字】

1.

2.
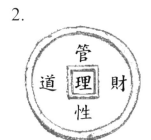

3.

字⇨　詞⇨　句⇨　文

1 確	正確	你的發音很**正確**。
	準確	這個方法的**準確**度很高。
	確認	請**確認**我訂的機票沒有問題。
	確定	我十分**確定**就是他。

　　你確定這些錢的數字正確嗎？要不要再確認一次，你一張一張數，又慢又容易錯，不如用點鈔機來算錢，又快又準確。

2 理	管理	經理就是要**管理**好大大小小的事情。
	道理	他做人很有道理，可是做事沒**道理**。
	理性	太生氣了就會失去**理性**。
	理財	要找**理財**專家幫你整理財產。

　　很多人沒有金錢管理的觀念，逛街買東西的時候不夠理性，因此常常花的錢比賺的錢多。對很多還沒出社會的年輕人來說，他們不懂賺錢辛苦的道理，父母有責任教導他們如何理財。

3 獨	單獨	太晚了！不要**單獨**一個人出去。
	孤獨	不要讓朋友**孤獨**地去面對問題。
	獨立	從小就習慣**獨立**，長大就能獨立處理問題。
	獨自	他**獨自**一個人在那裡喝酒，去陪陪他吧！

　　我是一個從小就很**獨立**的人，常常喜歡**單獨**一個人聽音樂、做事。我的朋友不多，可是都是談得來的好朋友，所以，我不覺得**孤獨**，只是比較喜歡那種**獨自**一個人的自由感覺。

【六·練習】

(1) 成語

成語是簡短有力的固定詞組，熟練它可以幫助你用最簡短的詞語表達你的意思。

例：一五一十　說明一個事情怎麼發生、為什麼發生的經過，從頭到尾很清楚地把時間、地點、人等等都說明白。請你把事情的經過_____地說出來。

1. 一帆風順　事情進行地很順利

2. 二人同心　團結的力量可以對付敵人

3. 三思而行　再三考慮之後再做

4. 四通八達　四方相通的道路

5. 五花八門　多形色、多變化

6. 六神無主　心神慌亂，沒辦法決定。

7. 七上八下　心情忐忑不安

8. 八九不離十　差不多！

9. 九牛一毛　多數中的極少部分，對大體沒有什麼影響。

10. 十全十美　圓滿美好

練習：請填入適當的成語
1. 百貨公司裡面的東西_____。
2. 祝你_____。
3. 天下沒有_____的事。
4. 你看我猜的是不是_____？
5. 這種小錢對有錢人來說是_____。
6. 我現在的心情是_____，不知道該怎麼辦？
7. 怎麼會發生這種事？我真是_____了。
8. 我們只要_____一定可以得第一名。
9. 這是大事，你要_____。
10. 高雄市的馬路_____，很好走。

（2）看圖說故事

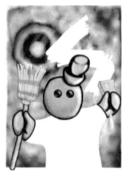

蔡光輝

1. A 跟 B 不能比，因為各有各的美。
2. 黑白圖跟彩色圖有甚麼差別？
3. 既然黑中有白，那麼白中也有黑吧！
4. 熱門的電影有很多人排隊看，冷門的呢？
5. 聰明的機器人，除了做複雜的工作之外，還可以做家事。

（1）办公大楼

欧福： 台湾的大楼都好高！这些都是办公室吗？

老师： 不一定，有些是纯办公大楼，有些是综合式的大楼。

德美： 什么是综合式的大楼？

得中： 我猜猜看。是不是有公司也有住家？

老师： 真聪明！一猜就猜中了。这些综合式的大楼里面有办公室、个人的工作室，也有住家。

德美： 那样不是很复杂吗？

老师： 的确很复杂，不认识也不知道邻居是做什么的。

欧福： 既然有纯办公大楼，那么也有纯住家大楼吗？

老师： 有，那些纯住家大楼，就单纯多了。看！就像那样的新社区，跟刚才的比起来是不是好多了。

（2）旧社区

老师： 你们看这附近的房子，跟我们刚才看的有什么不一样？

得中： 这一区的房子好像比较旧，也没那么高了。

老师： 这些就是比大楼更早期的公寓。

欧福： 除了新旧之外，还有什么不同吗？

老师： 公寓大多是五楼以下，没有电梯，也没有管理员。

德美： 哇！这一区的房子好漂亮啊！

老师： 这里是新的独门独户的别墅区。比比看！跟透天的房子有什么差别？

【八·拼音對照】

DÌ SHÍ ÈR KÈ　　CĀNGUĀN SHÈQŪ

（1）Bàngōng Dàlóu

Ōufú: 　Táiwān de dàlóu dōu hǎo gāo!　Zhèxiē dōu shì bàngōng shì ma?

Lǎoshī: 　Bù yídìng, yǒuxiē shì chún bàngōng dàlóu, yǒuxiē shì zònghé shì de dàlóu.

Déměi : Shéme shì zònghé shì de dàlóu?

Dézhōng : Wǒ cāicāikàn. Shìbúshì yǒu gōngsī yěyǒu zhùjiā?

Lǎoshī: Zhēn cōngmíng! Yìcāi jiù cāizhòng le. Zhèxiē zònghé shì de dàlóu lǐmiàn yǒu bàngōng shì, gèrén de gōngzuò shì, yěyǒu zhùjiā.

Déměi: Nàyàng búshì hěn fùzá ma?

Lǎoshī: Díquè hěn fùzá, bú rènshì yě bù zhīdào línjū shì zuò shéme de.

Ōufú: Jìrán yǒu chún bàngōng dàlóu, nàme yěyǒu chún zhùjiā dàlóu ma?

Lǎoshī: Yǒu, nàxiē chún zhùjiā dàlóu, jiù dānchún duō le. Kàn! Jiùxiàng nàyàng de xīn shèqū, gēn gāngcái de bǐ qǐlái shì búshì hǎo duō le .

(2) Jiù Shèqū.

Lǎoshī: Nǐmen kàn zhè fùjìn de fángzi, gēn wǒmen gāngcái kàn de yǒu shéme bù yíyàng?

Déměi: Zhè yìqū de fángzi hǎoxiàng bǐjiào jiù, yě méi nàme gāo le.

Lǎoshī: Zhè jiùshì bǐ dàlóu gèng zǎoqí de gōngyù.

Ōufú: Chúle xīnjiù zhīwài, háiyǒu shéme bùtóng ma?

Lǎoshī: Gōngyù dà duōshì wǔlóu yǐxià, méiyǒu diàntī, méiyǒu guǎnlǐ yuán.

Dézhōng: Wa! Zhèyìqū de fángzi hǎo piàoliàng a!

Lǎoshī: Zhèshì xīnde dúmén dúhù de biéshù qū. Bǐbǐ kàn! Gēn tòutiān de fángzi yǒu shéme chābié?

【九 · 英文翻譯】

◆ **Dialogue** – p. 162~163

(1) Office Buildings

Oufu: The buildings in Taiwan are all so tall! Are these all office buildings?

Teacher: Not necessarily. Some are entirely office buildings, and some are "mixed" buildings.

Demei: What are "mixed" buildings?

Dezhong: Let me guess. Do they have companies and family residences?

Teacher: Really clever! Right on the first guess! These "mixed" buildings combine offices, studios, and are also residential.

Demei: Isn't that kind of complicated?

Teacher: Of course it's complicated! None of the neighbors know each other, and they don't know what their neighbors do!

Oufu: Since there are buildings which are entirely office buildings, then are there any buildings which are entirely residential?

Teacher: Yes. Those buildings which are entirely residential are a lot less complicated! Hey, look! They're just like those residential communities! Much better in comparison to those mixed buildings and old apartments!

(2) An Older Community

Teacher: Look at the houses nearby, how are they different from the buildings we've just looked at?

Dezhong: The houses in this area look older, and they're not so tall.

Teacher: These are apartment buildings which were built much earlier than the taller buildings.

Oufu: Except for being older, how else are they different?

Teacher: The apartment buildings are all five stories or under, and none of them have elevators or superintendents.

Demei: Wow! The houses in this area are really pretty!

Teacher: This is an area with single unit dachas. You can compare these with the "tou tian" style buildings. How do they differ?

◆ **Vocabulary** – **p. 164~165**

1. family residence   This is a mixed style building, combining offices and residences.
2. mixed style   Let's order a combination salad.
3. smart, clever, intelligent   Smart is as smart does.

4.	to guess	Can you guess my age?
5.	complicated, complex	Don't over think it too much!
6.	office	Where is the teacher's office?
7.	pure	Is this one hundred percent pure fruit juice?
8.	studio	I'm thinking of converting this apartment into a studio.
9.	multi-storied house belonging to a single family	We can share the rent on a four-storey "tou tian" style house.
10.	since	Since you don't have time now, let's talk some other time!
11.	certain, sure	That surely is a smart way of doing it!
12.	neighbor	Let's go say "hello" to our neighbor.
13.	difference, discrepancy	What's the difference between these two drinks?
14.	nearby	Are there any apartments for rent nearby?
15.	single family unit	Single family unit houses are certainly expensive.
16.	dacha	We have a summer home in the countryside.
17.	community, neighborhood	That is a safe and quiet neighborhood.
18.	elevator	Don't take an elevator during an earthquake.
19.	early period	Early movies were in black and white.
20.	superintendent, janitor	The superintendent here has to take care of a lot of things.

◆ **Grammar** – p. 166

(1) …as soon as…

Q: Are motorcycles easy to ride?

A: Very easy!   Even easier than bicycles.

1. Is the exchange rate for Euros high?
2. Is it easy to find work now?
3. Has he gotten used to living abroad?

(2) …since…then…

Q: Do you really not have another girlfriend?

A: Since you ask me, then I'll tell you!

  1. Bought / use

  2. Lacking time / don't go

  3. Believe / don't ask him

(3) …compared with…

Q: How is Taiwan's weather?

A: Compared to Germany, it's a LOT hotter!

  1. How is this machine?   Made by hand / a lot more convenient

  2. How is this little garden?   Park / a lot smaller

  3. How was yesterday's homework?   Report / a little easier

(4) …except for /besides / in addition to, furthermore…

Q: How many cars does your family have?

A: In addition to these two, there's one more.

  1. Where can I withdraw money?   Bank / post office

  2. What's for after the meal?   Coffee / dessert

  3. You don't have a car, so how do you go to school?

    Bus / mass rapid transit

◆ **Word to Sentence** – p. 167

1 確	accurate, correct	Your pronunciation is very accurate.
	precise, exact	This method's level of precision is quite high.
	affirm, confirm, certify, identify	Please confirm that my airplane ticket doesn't have any problems.
	decide, fix, settle, certain, sure	I am quite certain that is him.

  Are you sure the amount of money is correct? Do you want to confirm that again? Counting each bill one by one is slow, and it's easy to make a mistake. It is not nearly as good as using a counting machine, which is both faster and more precise.

2 理	manage, handle, administer, administration	The manager's job is to administer all manner of business, no matter whether big or small.
	reason, rationality	He is a very rational and ethical person, but he's not good at handling practical matters.
	reason, sense, rationality	If you become too angry you will behave irrationally.
	manage or administer finances	Look for a professional to help you manage your finances.

Many people do not have any concept about managing their finances. When they go shopping they act like they don't have any sense. Consequently, they spend more than they earn.　Young people who haven't started working yet do not understand how hard it is to make money, so parents should teach them how to budget their finances.

3 獨	alone, single	It's too late!　Don't go out by yourself.
	alone, in solitude	Do not let your friends deal with problems alone.
	independent, self-reliant	If you are used to being self-reliant from childhood, you can deal with any problem on your own after you grow up.
	unaccompanied, alone, single-handed	He is over there drinking by himself.　Go keep him company!

When I was a child, I was very independent.　I liked listening to music and doing things by myself.　I didn't have a lot of friends, but the ones I had were good friends.　So, I didn't feel lonely.　I just preferred the freedom of being alone.

閱讀（三）

　　我來台灣才一個月，就交了三個台灣朋友，也一起去了不少地方。我對台灣的夜生活文化特別有興趣，所以和台灣朋友到高雄的夜市去逛逛。「夜市」的意思是晚上的市場。我們去了高雄市最有名的六合夜市，那裡的東西比別的夜市貴，我想是因為外地觀光客多的原因吧。

　　到了下午四、五點，六合路的兩邊開始擺攤子。有的攤子賣吃的，有的攤子賣穿的，真的是要什麼有什麼。我帶著數位照相機跟著台灣朋友逛，台灣人真能吃，一個攤子一個攤子地吃，真讓我大開眼界。我只吃烤肉、湯圓、和八寶冰，就已經不行了，本來也想吃有名的臭豆腐，但是臭豆腐實在太臭了，還是算了。

　　我在六合夜市買了五件 T 恤、兩個錢包和三雙筷子，沒花多少錢，因為跟老闆講價，<u>一點都沒吃虧</u>。我照了六十幾張照片，打算回宿舍寫有關台灣夜市的報告，傳給美國的家人和朋友，希望他們也能多瞭解台灣的夜生活文化。

　　越晚，夜市的人越多，也越來越熱鬧了。到底夜市有多麼好玩呢？我想只有去過的人，才知道它的樂趣吧！

1. 六合夜市為什麼東西比較貴？
2. 作者在夜市吃了什麼東西？
3. 作者說「<u>一點都沒吃虧</u>」是什麼意思？
4. 六合夜市賣些什麼東西？ 作者照相做什麼？

複習 （三）

一、生詞與語法

1.省錢	2.照顧	3.新鮮	4.看起來	5.各式各樣
6. 除了	7.剛	8.整理	9.還不如	10.三代同堂
11.複雜	12.立業	13.既然	14.獨門獨戶	15.討價還價

1. 外面下雨，逛街不方便，我覺得（　　）在家看電視好。

2. 這個菜（　　）很好吃，可是吃起來不太好吃。

3. 我的房間太小，東西太多，不好（　　）。

4. 夜市有（　　）的攤子，有吃的，有喝的，也有很多日用品。

5. 小林是家中的老大，所以媽媽忙的時候，要（　　）弟弟妹妹。

6. 都市人口多，房子小，（　　）的情形越來越少了。

7. 畢了業，我想先（　　）再成家。

8. 都市車子多，空氣不好。山上就不一樣了，空氣非常（　　）。

9. 我的中文說得不好，所以買東西的時候，不會（　　）。

10. （　　）你不喝這杯咖啡，就給我喝吧。

11. 你（　　）會說英文、中文之外，還會說哪一種語言？

12. 台北房子貴，土地更貴，一般人是住不起（　　）的房子。

13. 這件事情，從外面看起來好像很單純，其實非常的（　　）。

14. 他很年輕就結婚了，沒錢，想（　　），所以跟父母住在一起。

15. 我（　　）吃過麵包，現在吃不下飯了，只想喝「珍珠奶茶」。

附　錄

謝逸娥　繪

A

ài sǐ	愛死	爱死	V.	6
ānquán	安全	安全	Adj.	5

B

bàn shìqíng	辦事情	办事情	V.	7
bàngōng	辦公	办公	V.	12
bǎo	飽	饱	Adj.	3
bǎomǔ	保母	保母	N.	10
běnlái	本來	本来	Adj.	3
biéshù	別墅	别墅	N.	12
bù kěnéng	不可能	不可能	Adj.	2
bǔchōng	補充	补充	V.	9
bùlǐ	不理	不理	V.	11
bùquán	不全	不全	Adj.	9
bǔxí	補習	补习	V.	9
bùzhǐ	不只	不只	Adv.	7

C

cāi	猜	猜	V.	12
chá	查	查	V.	9
chābié	差別	差別	N.	12
chāojí shìchǎng	超級市場	超级市场	N.	11
chéngjiā lìyè	成家立業	成家立业	V.	10
chénglì	成立	成立	V.	10
chéngnián	成年	成年	Adj.	4
chéngyǔ	成語	成语	N.	10
chīkuī	吃虧	吃亏	V.	4
chuántǒng shìchǎng	傳統市場	传统市场	N.	11
chún	純	纯	Adj.	12
cōngmíng	聰明	聪明	Adj.	12
cúnqián	存錢	存钱	V.	10

D

dàbùfèn	大部分	大部分	Adj.	11
dàgài	大概	大概	Adv.	10
dài	帶	带	V.	6
dài ānquán mào	戴安全帽	戴安全帽	V.	7
dàjiā	大家	大家	N.	2
dānchún	單純	单纯	Adj.	1
dāngrán	當然	当然	Adv.	5
dàochù	到處	到处	Adj.	3
dǎoyóu	導遊	导游	N.	5
dàyuē	大約	大约	Adv.	1
dédào	得到	得到	N.	2
diàntī	電梯	电梯	N.	12
dìfāng	地方	地方	N.	1
díquè	的確	的确	Adj.	12
dìtú	地圖	地图	N.	5
dǒngshì	懂事	懂事	Adj.	6
dúméndúhù	獨門獨戶	独门独户	Adj.	12
duōjiǔ	多久	多久	Adj.	2
dūshì	都市	都市	N.	7
dùzǐ	肚子	肚子	N.	3

E

érqiě	而且	而且	Conj.	11

F

fēngjǐng	風景	风景	N.	5
fùjìn	附近	附近	N.	12
fúqì	福氣	福气	N.	2
fùzá	複雜	复杂	Adj.	12

G

gǎitiān	改天	改天	N.	3
gāng	剛	刚	Adv.	9

gānjìng	乾淨	干净	Adj.	11
gèmáng gède	各忙各的	各忙各的	Adj.	11
gōngzuò	工作	工作	N.	1
gōngzuòshì	工作室	工作室	N.	12
guānchá	觀察	观察	N./V.	7
guānguāng	觀光	观光	N./ V.	1
guǎnlǐyuán	管理員	管理员	N.	12
guānniàn	觀念	观念	N.	10
guānxi	關係	关系	N.	8
guìtái	櫃台	柜台	N.	4
Guóyǔ	國語	国语	N.	1

H

hǎidǎo	海島	海岛	N.	1
háishì	還是	还是	Adv.	2
hàomǎjī	號碼機	号码机	N.	4
hǎoxiǎn	好險	好险	Adj.	7
hǎoxiàng	好像	好像	Adv.	8
hòulái	後來	后来	Adj.	3
hù zhào	護照	护照	N.	4
huà shì méicuò	話是沒錯	话是没错	Adj.	11
huándǎo	環島	环岛	Adj.	5
huángdì	皇帝	皇帝	N.	8
huānyíng	歡迎	欢迎	V.	8
huí qǐng	回請	回请	V.	3
huìlǜ	匯率	汇率	N.	4
hùxiāng	互相	互相	Adv.	10

J

jiǎngjià	講價	讲价	V.	11
jiǎnjiè	簡介	简介	N.	5
jiǎntǐ zì	簡體字	简体字	N.	2
jiànyì	建議	建议	N.	5
jiāohuàn	交換	交换	V.	4

jiāotōng	交通	交通	Adj.	7
jiàoyù	教育	教育	N.	9
jiàqián	價錢	价钱	N.	4
jiāshàng	加上	加上	Adv.	8
jiātíng	家庭	家庭	N.	6
jīběn	基本	基本	Adj.	9
jiēdài	接待	接待	V.	6
jiēfēng	接風	接风	V.	3
jiéhūn	結婚	结婚	V.	10
jièshào	介紹	介绍	V.	2
jiēsòng	接送	接送	V.	7
jījīng	雞精	鸡精	N.	9
jīngshén	精神	精神	N.	9
jìrán	既然	既然	Conj.	12
jiùmìng	救命	救命	V.	7

K				
kāixīn	開心	开心	V.	6
Kěndīng	墾丁	垦丁	N.	6
kěpà	可怕	可怕	Adj.	7
kèqì	客氣	客气	Adj.	2
kèqìhuà	客氣話	客气话	N.	8
kǒuwèi	口味	口味	N.	6

L				
lǎn	懶	懒	Adj.	9
làngfèi	浪費	浪费	V.	7
lǐmào	禮貌	礼貌	Adj.	6
línjū	鄰居	邻居	N.	12
lǐwù	禮物	礼物	N.	8
lǚxíng	旅行	旅行	V.	5

M				
mílù	迷路	迷路	V.	5

mótuōchē	摩托車	摩托车	N.	7
mùdì	目的	目的	N.	1

N				
nánguài	難怪	难怪	Adv.	8
niánqīng	年輕	年轻	Adj.	10

O				
Ōuzhōu	歐洲	欧洲	N.	2

P				
pà	怕	怕	V.	5
piàoliàng	漂亮	漂亮	Adj.	2
píngcháng	平常	平常	Adj.	11

Q				
qí guài	奇怪	奇怪	Adj.	4
qìfēn	氣氛	气氛	N.	3
qīngchǔ	清楚	清楚	Adj.	4
qīngsōng	輕鬆	轻松	Adj.	3
qǐngwèn	請問	请问	VP.	1
qíngxíng	情形	情形	N.	5
qiú zhī bù dé	求之不得	求之不得	Adj.	6
quēshǎo	缺少	缺少	Adj.	9
quèshí	確實	确实	Adj.	7

R				
ràng	讓	让	V.	3
rènào	熱鬧	热闹	Adj.	8
rénkǒu	人口	人口	N.	1
rénqíng wèi	人情味	人情味	N.	11
rènshì	認識	认识	V.	2

S

sāndài	三代	三代	N.	10
sāndài tóngtáng	三代同堂	三代同堂	V.	10
sānmíngzhì	三明治	三明治	N.	6
shàngwǎng	上網	上网	V.	9
shěngqián	省錢	省钱	V.	10
shēngyì	生意	生意	N.	1
shēngyīn	聲音	声音	N.	8
shèqū	社區	社区	N.	12
shíduàn	時段	时段	N.	7
shīlǐ	失禮	失礼	Adj.	3
shìqū	市區	市区	N.	7
shóu	熟	熟	Adj.	5
shōuxià	收下	收下	V.	8
shūfú	舒服	舒服	Adj.	5
shuǐfèn	水份	水份	N.	9
shùnbiàn	順便	顺便	Adj.	7
sòng	送	送	V.	8
suàn	算	算	V.	11

T

tānzi	攤子	摊子	N.	11
tǎojià huánjià	討價還價	讨价还价	V.	11
tèbié	特別	特别	Adj.	8
tì	替	替	V.	3
tiánbiǎo	填表	填表	V.	4
tíngchēwèi	停車位	停车位	N.	7
tīngshuō	聽說	听说	V.	5
tóngshí	同時	同时	Adv.	10
tóngxué	同學	同学	N.	2
tòutiān	透天	透天	Adj.	12
tǔ shēng tǔ zhǎng	土生土長	土生土长	Adj.	5

W				
wàibì	外幣	外币	N.	4
wéitāmìng	維他命	维他命	N.	9
wéixiǎn	危險	危险	Adj.	7
wénhuà	文化	文化	N.	1
wúliáo	無聊	无聊	Adj.	4

X				
xiàndài	現代	现代	N.	10
xiǎochī	小吃	小吃	N.	3
xiāoxí	消息	消息	N.	6
xiàyítiào	嚇一跳	吓一跳	V.	7
xíguàn	習慣	习惯	N.	5
xìngfú	幸福	幸福	Adj.	10
xìngqù	興趣	兴趣	N.	1
xīnxiān	新鮮	新鲜	Adj.	11
xīnyì	心意	心意	N.	3
xiūlǚ chē	休旅車	休旅车	N.	6
xuǎnzé	選擇	选择	N. V.	11
xūyào	需要	需要	N. V.	1

Y				
yǎnjīng	眼睛	眼睛	N.	3
yánjiùsuǒ	研究所	研究所	N.	9
yèshì	夜市	夜市	N.	3
yídàzǎo	一大早	一大早	Adj.	11
Yīngwén	英文	英文	N.	1
yínháng	銀行	银行	N.	4
yǐnliào	飲料	饮料	N.	4
yīshī	醫師	医师	N.	9
yíyàng	一樣	一样	Adj.	2
yóu jià	油價	油价	N.	6
yóu qián	油錢	油钱	N.	6
yuányīn	原因	原因	N.	11

yuánzhùmín	原住民	原住民	N.	5

Z

zǎoqí	早期	早期	Adj.	12
zhànpiányí	佔便宜	占便宜	V.	4
zhàogù	照顧	照顾	V.	10
zhěnglǐ	整理	整理	V.	9
zhèngquè	正確	正确	Adj.	7
zhèngtǐ zì	正體字	正体字	N.	2
zhòngdiǎn	重點	重点	N.	9
zhòngshì	重視	重视	Adj.	3
Zhōngwén	中文	中文	N.	1
zhòngyào	重要	重要	Adj.	3
zhòngyào	重要	重要	Adj.	8
zhōumò	週末	周末	N.	6
zhùjiā	住家	住家	N.	12
zhǔnbèi	準備	准备	V.	8
zīliào	資料	资料	N.	9
zìyóu	自由	自由	Adj.	5
zònghéshì	綜合式	综合式	Adj.	12
zū chē	租車	租车	V.	5
zuǐbā	嘴巴	嘴巴	N.	3
zuìjìn	最近	最近	Adv.	1
zuòshì	做事	做事	V.	8
zuòwèi	座位	座位	N.	6
zuòyè	作業	作业	N.	2

語法索引

第一課　一二三到台灣	
1.	…（倒）是…可是…	班上會說德文的人，有倒是有，可是很少。
2.	…越來越…	我最近越來越忙了。
3.	有的…有的…	在台灣，有的人說國語，有的人說台語。
4.	對…很有興趣	我對寫漢字很有興趣。

第二課　自我介紹	
5.	…的…，…的…	A：請問「事先」怎麼寫？ B：事情的事，先生的先。
6.	…得…，是…的？	你的中文說得很好，是在哪裡學的？
7.	…跟…一樣	我要吃跟他一樣的東西。
8.	…了…了， 可是還是不（太）…	我學中文學了一年了，可是還是不太會說。

第三課　飲食文化	
9.	…什麼…都/也…	他生病了，什麼東西都吃不下。
10.	…來不及…	老師說話說得太快了，我都來不及聽。
11.	本來…，後來…	我本來要去上海，後來決定來台灣。
12.	讓…，真的…	讓你花那麼多錢，真的很不好意思。

第四課　我需要換台幣	
13.	只有…才…	只有當地人才知道哪裡有好吃的餐廳。
14.	帶著…，到…	帶著你的護照跟我去圖書館申請借書證。
15.	每…	我每一個星期上五天中文課。
16.	要…，就…。 不要…太多。	你要吃多少，就拿多少，不要一次拿太多。

第五課 遊山玩水		
17.	從…到…	從高雄開車到台南,差不多半個小時。
18.	…是…,可是…	A:你喜歡台灣菜嗎? B:喜歡是喜歡,可是太油了。
19.	對…不熟	我對這個軟體不熟。
20.	還是…比較…	我覺得還是開車去玩比較方便。

第六課 接待家庭		
21.	…過…沒?	我們星期六去旅行,你問過你的家人沒?
22.	不是…的問題, 是…(上)的問題	我不能去旅行,不是錢的問題,是時間上的問題。
23.	禮貌上先…一下	你去朋友家以前,禮貌上先打一下電話比較好。
24.	…,一定…死…了	你家來了十個小孩,一定吵死你了。

第七課 台灣的交通		
25.	…是不是…? 好像還不只…	A:我們以前是不是見過? B:對,好像還不只一次。
26.	…,…確實…	中文確實難學。
27.	…沒…又…,好…!	他沒戴安全帽又騎得那麼快,好危險!
28.	…好…,準備…了	整理好行李,準備出門了。

第八課 吃飯皇帝大		
29.	…跟… 有/沒(有)關係	這件事跟他沒有關係。
30.	…好像…一樣	他寫的漢字好像老師寫的一樣。
31.	…(沒)有什麼	今天家裡沒有什麼好吃的菜。
32.	…因為…,再加上…	我今天沒去考試是因為生病了, 再加上這幾天忙,沒看書。

第九課	補補補！	
33.	…一點都不/沒…	我一點都不想去看電影。
34.	對…來說， 那是不可能…	六點起床，對懶人來說，那是不可能的事情。
35.	除了…之外，還…。	除了加強會話能力之外，還想學書法。
36.	看來…了！	看來他今天不會來了！

第十課	三代同堂	
37.	…看起來…	這件事情看起來很複雜。
38.	不一定，要看…	A：學生都不喜歡做功課嗎？ B：不一定，要看是什麼功課。
39.	…了…，…了…， 就可以…了。	我畢了業，存夠了錢，就可以出國唸書了。
40.	…，還不如…	找人幫忙，還不如自己做。

第十一課	傳統與現代	
41.	…，而且…	她是一位好媽媽，而且還是一位好老師。
42.	話是沒錯，可是…。	A：我覺得在超市買菜比較好。 B：話是沒錯，可是我還是習慣傳統市場。
43.	…比…多了。	超級市場比傳統市場乾淨多了。
44.	…，一方面…， 一方面…。	去傳統市場買菜，一方面可以講價，一方面可以學中文。

第十二課	參觀社區	
45.	比…更…	摩托車比腳踏車更好騎。
46.	既然…就…	既然你問了，我就告訴你吧。
47.	跟…比起來	台灣跟日本比起來，熱多了。
48.	除了…之外，還有…	我除了有腳踏車之外，還有一輛摩托車。

	筆劃	部首	古字	讀音	意思	例字
1.	1	一	一	yī	one	上
2.	1	乙	ㄟ	yǐ	bent	九
3.	2	二	二	èr	two	五
4.	2	人	入	rén	man	他
5.	2	入	入	rù	enter	兩
6.	2	八	八	bā	eight	公
7.	2	刀	刀	dāo	knife	分
8.	2	力	力	lì	strength	加
9.	2	勹	○	bāo	wrap	包
10.	2	十	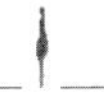 ┃	shí	ten	千
11.	2	又	ㄋ	yòu	also	友
12.	3	口	ㅂ	kǒu	mouth	吃
13.	3	囗	□	wéi	enclosure	國
14.	3	土	土	tǔ	earth	地
15.	3	士	士	shì	scholar	壯
16.	3	夕	ㄗ	xì	evening	外
17.	3	大	大	dà	great	太
18.	3	女	大	nǔ	woman	媽
19.	3	子	ㄓ	zi	child	孩
20.	3	宀	介	mián	roof	家
21.	3	寸	�	cùn	inch	對
22.	3	小	川	xiǎo	small	少
23.	3	尸	尸	shī	corpse	尾
24.	3	山	山	shān	mountain	岩
25.	3	工	工	gōng	work	左
26.	3	己	己	jǐ	self	巴

	筆劃	部首	古字	讀音	意思	例字
27.	3	巾		jīn	napkin	市
28.	3	干		gān	shield	平
29.	3	幺		yāo	tiny	幾
30.	3	广		yǎn	shelter	床
31.	3	弓		gōng	a bow	張
32.	3	彡		shān	feathery	形
33.	3	彳		chì	to pace	後
34.	4	心		xīn	heart	愛我
35.	4	戈		gē	spear	我
36.	4	戶		hù	door	房
37.	4	手		shǒu	hand	打
38.	4	支		zhī	branch	支
39.	4	攴		pū	tap	收
40.	4	文		wén	writing	文
41.	4	斗		dǒu	measure	料
42.	4	斤		jīn	axe	新
43.	4	方		fāng	square	旁
44.	4	日		rì	sun	旦
45.	4	曰		yuē	speak	書
46.	4	月		yuè	moon	朋
47.	4	木		mù	wood	林
48.	4	欠		qiàn	owe	次
49.	4	止		zhǐ	stop	正
50.	4	歹		dǎi	evil	死
51.	4	比		bǐ	compare	比
52.	4	毛		máo	hair	毫
53.	4	氏		shì	family	民
54.	4	气		qì	air	氣

	筆劃	部首	古字	讀音	意思	例字
55.	4	水		shuǐ	water	池
56.	4	火		huǒ	fire	煮
57.	4	爪		zhǎo	claws	爬
58.	4	片		piàn	a strip	牌
59.	4	牛		niú	ox	特
60.	4	犬		quǎn	dog	狗
61.	5	玄		xuán	dark	率
62.	5	玉		yù	jade	玫
63.	5	瓜		guā	melon	瓜
64.	5	甘		gān	sweet	甜
65.	5	生		shēng	produce	產
66.	5	用		yòng	use	甩
67.	5	田		tián	field	甲
68.	5	疒		chuáng	sick	病
69.	5	癶		bō	back to back	發
70.	5	白		bái	white	百
71.	5	皮		pí	skin	皮
72.	5	目		mù	eye	眼
73.	5	矛		máo	lance	矛
74.	5	矢		shǐ	arrow	知
75.	5	石		shí	stone	碗
76.	5	示		shì	spirit	禮
77.	5	禾		hé	grain	秋
78.	5	穴		xuè	cave	穿
79.	5	立		lì	erect	站
80.	6	竹		zhú	bamboo	篁

	筆劃	部首	古字	讀音	意思	例字
81.	6	米		mǐ	rice	粽
82.	6	糸		mì	silk	絲
83.	6	网		wǎng	net	置
84.	6	羊		yáng	sheep	美
85.	6	羽		yǔ	feathers	翁
86.	6	老		lǎo	old	考
87.	6	而		ér	and	耐
88.	6	耳		ěr	ear	聽
89.	6	肉		ròu	flesh	胖
90.	6	自		zì	self/ from	臭
91.	6	至		zhì	reach	臺
92.	6	舌		shé	tongue	舒
93.	6	舟		zhōu	boat	船
94.	6	色		sè	color	色
95.	6	艸		cǎo	grass	菜
96.	6	虫		huǐ	insect	蟲
97.	6	血		xiě	blood	血
98.	6	行		xíng	go, do	街
99.	6	衣		yī	clothes	裡
100.	7	見		jiàn	see	觀
101.	7	角		jiǎo	horn	角
102.	7	言		yán	words	說
103.	7	谷		gǔ	valley	谷
104.	7	豆		dòu	platter/bean	豆
105.	7	豕		shǐ	pig	貓
106.	7	貝		bèi	shell	貨
107.	7	赤		chì	red	赤
108.	7	走		zǒu	walk	起

	筆劃	部首	古字	讀音	意思	例字
109.	7	足		zú	foot	跑
110.	7	身		shēn	body	躺
111.	7	車		chē	cart	輪
112.	7	辵		chuò	stop & go	遊
113.	7	邑		yì	city	那
114.	7	酉		yǒu	new wine	醜
115.	7	里		lǐ	village	重
116.	8	金		jīn	metal	針
117.	8	長		cháng	long	長
118.	8	門		mén	gate	開
119.	8	阜		fù	plenty	限
120.	8	隹		zhuī	bird	雙
121.	8	雨		yǔ	rain	雪
122.	8	青		qīng	azure	靜
123.	8	非		fēi	false	靠
124.	9	面		miàn	face	面
125.	9	革		gé	rawhide	鞋
126.	9	音		yīn	sound	響
127.	9	頁		yè	heading	頂
128.	9	風		fēng	wind	颱
129.	9	飛		fēi	fly	飛
130.	9	食		shí	eat	飯
131.	9	首		shǒu	head	首
132.	9	香		xiāng	fragrance	香
133.	10	馬		mǎ	horse	馮
134.	10	骨		gǔ	bone	體
135.	10	高		gāo	high	高
136.	10	鬥		dòu	fight	鬧

	筆劃	部首	古字	讀音	意思	例字
137.	10	鬼		guǐ	ghost	魂
138.	11	魚		yú	fish	鮮
139.	11	鳥		niǎo	bird	鳳
140.	11	鹿		lù	deer	麈
141.	11	麥		mài	wheat	麵
142.	11	麻		má	hemp	麼
143.	12	黃		huáng	yellow	黃
144.	12	黑		hēi	black	點
145.	13	鼠		shǔ	rodent	鼠
146.	14	鼻		bí	nose	鼾

序號	筆劃	漢字	讀音	意思	例字
1.	一	橫	héng	horizontal lines	下三
1-a.	乛	橫折	héng zhé	right angle	日口
1-b.	乛	橫撇	héng piě	acute angle	又友
1-c.	乛	橫鈎	héng gōu	horizontal hook	也安
1-d.	乛	橫折鈎	héng zhé gōu	curve hook	的用
1-e.	乁	橫斜鈎	héng xié gōu	curve hook	九風
2.	丨	直	zhí	vertical lines	中申
2-a.	亅	豎鈎	shù gōu	vertical hook	小水
2-b.	亅	豎挑	shù tiǎo	vertical hook	衣食
2-c.	乚	豎曲鈎	shù qū gōu	curve hook	先花
3.	丶	點	diǎn	dots	六寸
4.	丿	撇	piě	sweep to the left	人父
5.	乀	捺	nà	sweep to the right	大足
6.	乀	挑	tiǎo	upward	冷冰
7.	乚	臥鈎	wò gōu	curve hook	心想
8.	乀	斜鈎	xié gōu	curve hook	我找

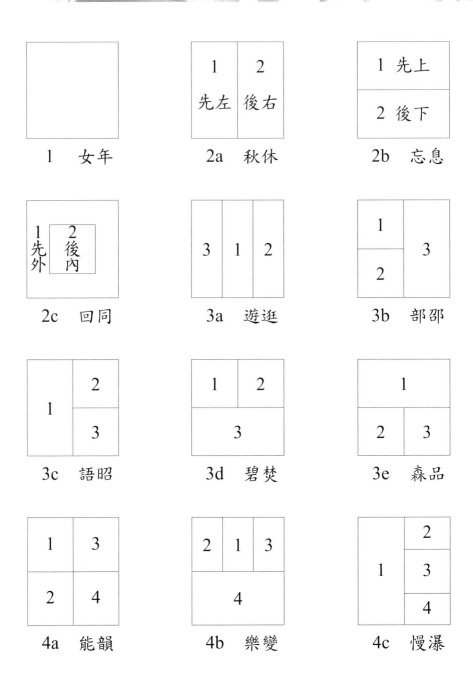

1　　女年

2a　　秋休

2b　　忘息

2c　　回同

3a　　遊逛

3b　　部邵

3c　　語昭

3d　　碧焚

3e　　森品

4a　　能韻

4b　　樂變

4c　　慢瀑

注音符號、漢語拼音對照表

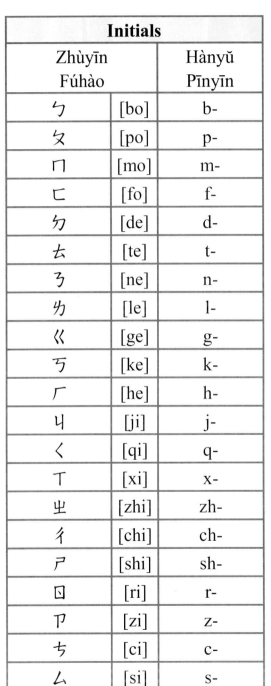

Initials		
Zhùyīn Fúhào		Hànyǔ Pīnyīn
ㄅ	[bo]	b-
ㄆ	[po]	p-
ㄇ	[mo]	m-
ㄈ	[fo]	f-
ㄉ	[de]	d-
ㄊ	[te]	t-
ㄋ	[ne]	n-
ㄌ	[le]	l-
ㄍ	[ge]	g-
ㄎ	[ke]	k-
ㄏ	[he]	h-
ㄐ	[ji]	j-
ㄑ	[qi]	q-
ㄒ	[xi]	x-
ㄓ	[zhi]	zh-
ㄔ	[chi]	ch-
ㄕ	[shi]	sh-
ㄖ	[ri]	r-
ㄗ	[zi]	z-
ㄘ	[ci]	c-
ㄙ	[si]	s-

Finals	
Zhùyīn Fúhào	Hànyǔ Pīnyīn
ㄚ	a
ㄛ	o
ㄜ	e
ㄝ	ê
ㄞ	ai
ㄟ	ei
ㄠ	ao
ㄡ	ou
ㄢ	an
ㄣ	en
ㄤ	ang
ㄥ	eng
ㄦ	er
ㄧ	yi/i
ㄨ	wu/-u
ㄩ	yu/-ü

Finals		Finals with "ㄧ"		Finals with "ㄨ"		Finals with "ㄩ"	
Zhù yīn	Pīnyīn	Zhù yīn	Pīnyīn	Zhù yīn	Pīnyīn	Zhù yīn	Pīnyīn
ㄚ	a	ㄧㄚ	ya/-ia	ㄨㄚ	wa/-ua		
ㄛ	o	ㄧㄛ	yo	ㄨㄛ	wo/-uo		
ㄜ	e						
ㄝ	ê	ㄧㄝ	ye/-ie			ㄩㄝ	yue/-üe
ㄞ	ai	ㄧㄞ	yai	ㄨㄞ	wai/-uai		
ㄟ	ei			ㄨㄟ	wei/-ui		
ㄠ	ao	ㄧㄠ	yao/-iao				
ㄡ	ou	ㄧㄡ	you/-iu				
ㄢ	an	ㄧㄢ	yan/-ian	ㄨㄢ	wan/-uan	ㄩㄢ	yuan/-üan
ㄣ	en	ㄧㄣ	yen/-in	ㄨㄣ	wen/-un	ㄩㄣ	yun/-ün
ㄤ	ang	ㄧㄤ	yang.-iang	ㄨㄤ	wang/-uang		
ㄥ	eng	ㄧㄥ	ying/-ing	ㄨㄥ	weng/-ong	ㄩㄥ	yong/-iong

Tones	Zhùyīn Fúhào	Hànyǔ Pīnyīn
1st tone		—
2nd tone	╱	╱
3rd tone	∨	∨
4th tone	╲	╲
Neutral tone	●	

文藻川菜・台菜館
菜　單

青椒牛肉 ……………	大 320 元	中 250 元	小 180 元
椒鹽里肌 ……………	大 300 元	中 220 元	小 150 元
宮保雞丁 ……………	大 300 元	中 220 元	小 150 元
北京烤鴨 ……………	大 450 元	中 350 元	小 250 元
糖醋魚 ………………	大 320 元	中 250 元	小 180 元
腰果蝦仁 ……………	大 280 元	中 200 元	小 130 元
麻婆豆腐 ……………	大 280 元	中 200 元	小 130 元
開洋白菜 ……………	大 300 元	中 220 元	小 160 元
炒青菜 ………………	大 250 元	中 180 元	小 120 元
螞蟻上樹 ……………	大 260 元	中 190 元	小 130 元
酸辣湯 ………………	大 250 元	中 180 元	小 120 元
海鮮羹 ………………	大 250 元	中 180 元	小 120 元

合菜：（附水果）

三菜一湯 ……………	999 元
四菜一湯 ……………	1199 元
五菜一湯 ……………	1299 元
六菜一湯 ……………	1499 元

電話：（07）3426031
傳真：（07）3426029
地址：高雄市三民區民族一路 900 號

遊學小站 茶飲連鎖專賣店			►OPEN TIME 10:00~22:00	
飲料名稱	**中**	**大**	**糖**	**冰**
綠茶	15	25	☐無☐半☐少	☐少☐去
紅茶	15	25	☐無☐半☐少	☐少☐去
奶茶	25	30	☐無☐半☐少	☐少☐去
百香綠/紅茶	30	45	☐無☐半☐少	☐少☐去
椰果綠/紅茶	35	55	☐無☐半☐少	☐少☐去
布丁奶茶	45	65	☐無☐半☐少	☐少☐去
多多綠茶	45	55	☐無☐半☐少	☐少☐去
綠奶茶	45	55	☐無☐半☐少	☐少☐去
鮮奶茶	30	45	☐無☐半☐少	☐少☐去
椰果奶茶	45	65	☐無☐半☐少	☐少☐去
(大/小)珍珠奶茶	45	65	☐無☐半☐少	☐少☐去
金桔檸檬	55	65	☐無☐半☐少	☐少☐去
冰/熱咖啡	45	65	☐無☐半☐少	☐少☐去

全面買五送一　　外送恕不優惠

老闆：「您好，要喝什麼？」
客人：「我要一杯綠茶。」
老闆：「冰塊、糖都正常嗎？」
客人：「我要少冰、半糖。」
老闆：「好，二十五元，收您三十元，找您五元，謝謝。」
客人：「謝謝。」

遊學快餐

滿兩百元可外送 (07)5252522

807 高雄市三民區鼎中路 1500 號

☐外帶 ☐內用　桌號：＿＿＿

美味快餐	價格	加 10 元
排骨飯	$75	☐加飯 ☐加滷蛋
雞腿飯	$85	☐加飯 ☐加滷蛋
魚排飯	$90	☐加飯 ☐加滷蛋
雞排飯	$75	☐加飯 ☐加滷蛋
燒肉飯	$80	☐加飯 ☐加滷蛋
宮保雞丁飯	$90	☐加飯 ☐加滷蛋
素食	任選三樣素菜、兩樣素肉	

老闆：「您好，要吃什麼？」
客人：「您好，我要一個雞腿飯外帶。」
老闆：「請選三種菜。」
客人：「我要這個、這個和那個。」
老闆：「八十五元。歡迎再來！」

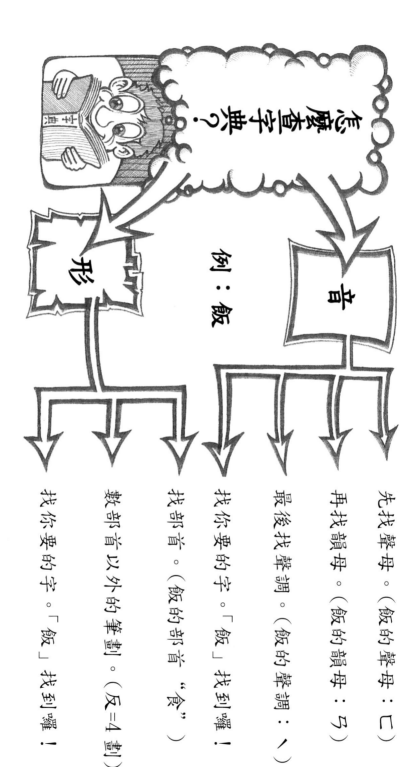

怎麼查字典？

音

例：飯

形

先找聲母。（飯的聲母：ㄈ）

再找韻母。（飯的韻母：ㄢ）

最後找聲調。（飯的聲調：ˋ）

找你要的字「飯」找到囉！

找部首。（飯的部首 “食”）

數部首以外的筆劃。（反＝4劃）

找你要的字。「飯」找到囉！

 參考文獻

一 · 華語文教學規範與理論基礎
　　　葉德明/師大書苑

二 · 漢字教學的理論與實踐
　　　黃沛榮/樂學書局

三 · 中央研究院　文獻處理實驗室
　　　http://www.sinica.edu.tw/~cdp/

四 · 中華民國教育部　國字筆畫併類表
　　　http://140.111.1.40/fulu/fu13/fubiau/bihua.htm

五 · 數位典藏國家型科技計畫
　　　http://www.ndap.org.tw/

六 · 教育部全球資訊網
　　　http://www.edu.tw

七 · 台灣觀光資訊網
　　　http://www.taiwan.net.tw/

八 · 交通部全球資訊網
　　　http://www.motc.gov.tw/

九 · 行政院青輔會青年旅遊網
　　　http://youthtravel.tw/youthtravel/indexMain.jsp

十 · 高雄旅遊資訊網
　　　http://www.kcg.gov.tw/travel/

跋

　　從事華語教學三十多年，由玩票兼職到專司行政，又再回到純教學；從台灣教到美國，再回到台灣，又是十數年，筆者一直樂在教學。每回領薪水，都覺得付學費、說感謝的人應該是我。這些渴望學中文的學生幫我開啟了一扇窗；他們的熱忱喚醒了我的熱情，又藉由他們好奇的眼，映出了台灣的美好。

　　全球數位學習蓬勃發展，改變傳統教材設計觀點，製作互動光碟，提供網路自學軟體等，乃當務之急。今因應時勢，以另類學習方式編纂《遊學華語》，期能拋磚引玉，帶出更多的創意教材問世。個人才疏學淺，編書經驗不足，尚祈各界先進不吝指教，共同為傳揚華夏語言文化而努力。

　　感謝文藻外語大學的支持及教育部卓越計畫的經費補助，謝謝師大華研所葉德明老師為本書提供寶貴意見，本校華語中心前主任廖南雁老師以及現任主任廖淑慧老師的精神鼓舞，編輯團隊姜君芳、葉亭妤、林冠良、黃嬿婷全心全意的付出，Mr. JC BARTIMUS 的插圖與美編指導，文藻客座教授 Dr. RICHARD CORNELL 指導教材編纂理念，試教老師們熱心提出各種建議，以及中心同仁鄒夢蘭、黃尹莎的多方協助。沒有這些助力，就不會有《遊學華語》的完成，謹此表達本人最誠摯的謝意。

文藻外語大學
華語中心
龔三慧

釀語言12　PD0042

 遊學華語

作　　者	文藻外語大學華語中心　龔三慧
執行編輯	黃姣婷
責任編輯	杜國維
編輯團隊	姜君芳、葉亭妤、林冠良
英文翻譯	JC Bartimus
德文翻譯	Christian Richter
錄音人員	龔三慧、姜君芳、杜文棠、李和舫、葉亭妤、林冠良、袁丞威
插　　畫	JC Bartimus
圖文排版	江怡緻
封面設計	徐烈火
封面完稿	王嵩賀

出版策劃	釀出版
製作發行	秀威資訊科技股份有限公司
	114 台北市內湖區瑞光路76巷65號1樓
	電話：+886-2-2796-3638　傳真：+886-2-2796-1377
	服務信箱：service@showwe.com.tw
	http://www.showwe.com.tw
郵政劃撥	19563868　戶名：秀威資訊科技股份有限公司
展售門市	國家書店【松江門市】
	104 台北市中山區松江路209號1樓
	電話：+886-2-2518-0207　傳真：+886-2-2518-0778
網路訂購	秀威網路書店：http://www.bodbooks.com.tw
	國家網路書店：http://www.govbooks.com.tw
法律顧問	毛國樑　律師
總 經 銷	聯合發行股份有限公司
	231新北市新店區寶橋路235巷6弄6號4F
	電話：+886-2-2917-8022　傳真：+886-2-2915-6275

出版日期	2017年1月　BOD一版
定　　價	350元

Printed in Taiwan

國家圖書館出版品預行編目

遊學華語 / 文藻外語大學華語中心著. -- 一
版. -- 臺北市：釀出版, 2017.1
　　面；　公分. -- (釀語言；12)
　BOD版
　ISBN 978-986-445-158-6(平裝)

　1.漢語 2.讀本

802.86　　　　　　　　　　105018597

讀者回函卡

感謝您購買本書，為提升服務品質，請填妥以下資料，將讀者回函卡直接寄回或傳真本公司，收到您的寶貴意見後，我們會收藏記錄及檢討，謝謝！如您需要了解本公司最新出版書目、購書優惠或企劃活動，歡迎您上網查詢或下載相關資料：http:// www.showwe.com.tw

您購買的書名：＿＿＿＿＿＿＿＿＿＿＿＿＿＿＿＿＿＿＿＿＿＿＿

出生日期：＿＿＿＿＿年＿＿＿＿＿月＿＿＿＿＿日

學歷：□高中 (含) 以下　　□大專　　□研究所 (含) 以上

職業：□製造業　□金融業　□資訊業　□軍警　□傳播業　□自由業
　　　□服務業　□公務員　□教職　　□學生　□家管　　□其它＿＿＿

購書地點：□網路書店　□實體書店　□書展　□郵購　□贈閱　□其他

您從何得知本書的消息？

　□網路書店　□實體書店　□網路搜尋　□電子報　□書訊　□雜誌
　□傳播媒體　□親友推薦　□網站推薦　□部落格　□其他＿＿＿＿＿＿

您對本書的評價：（請填代號　1.非常滿意　2.滿意　3.尚可　4.再改進）

　封面設計＿＿＿　版面編排＿＿＿　內容＿＿＿　文／譯筆＿＿＿　價格＿＿＿

讀完書後您覺得：

　□很有收穫　□有收穫　□收穫不多　□沒收穫

對我們的建議：＿＿＿＿＿＿＿＿＿＿＿＿＿＿＿＿＿＿＿＿＿＿＿

＿＿＿＿＿＿＿＿＿＿＿＿＿＿＿＿＿＿＿＿＿＿＿＿＿＿＿＿＿＿＿＿＿

＿＿＿＿＿＿＿＿＿＿＿＿＿＿＿＿＿＿＿＿＿＿＿＿＿＿＿＿＿＿＿＿＿

＿＿＿＿＿＿＿＿＿＿＿＿＿＿＿＿＿＿＿＿＿＿＿＿＿＿＿＿＿＿＿＿＿

11466
台北市內湖區瑞光路 76 巷 65 號 1 樓
秀威資訊科技股份有限公司 　　收
BOD 數位出版事業部

....

（請沿線對折寄回，謝謝！）

姓　　名：＿＿＿＿＿＿＿＿＿　年齡：＿＿＿＿＿　性別：□女　□男

郵遞區號：□□□□□

地　　址：＿＿＿＿＿＿＿＿＿＿＿＿＿＿＿＿＿＿＿＿＿＿＿＿

聯絡電話：(日)＿＿＿＿＿＿＿＿＿＿＿　(夜)＿＿＿＿＿＿＿＿＿＿＿

E-mail：＿＿＿＿＿＿＿＿＿＿＿＿＿＿＿＿＿＿＿＿＿＿